THE THREE-CORNERED HAT

THE
THREE-CORNERED
HAT

PEDRO ANTONIO de ALARCÓN

TRANSLATED BY H. F. TURNER

JOHN CALDER . LONDON

FIRST PUBLISHED IN THIS TRANSLATION IN 1959 BY
JOHN CALDER (PUBLISHERS) LTD
17 SACKVILLE STREET
LONDON W1
FROM THE SPANISH *El Sombrero de Tres Picos*

PRINTED IN GREAT BRITAIN BY
THE DITCHLING PRESS, HASSOCKS

CONTENTS

Introduction   1

Chronological Notes   7

Author's Preface   9

Chapter

I When it all Happened   13

II How they lived in those 'Good
   Old Days'   16

III A Sprat for a Mackerel   18

IV One Glance at a Woman   21

V A Glance all round—and in-
  side—a Man   25

VI A Married Couple's Aptitudes   27

VII The Foundations of Happiness   30

VIII The Man in the Three-
     cornered Hat   32

IX Get Along, Neddy!   36

X From the Trellis   38

XI The Bombardment of Pam-
   plona   42

XII Tithes and First Fruits   49

XIII Said the Jackdaw to the Raven   53

XIV Advice from The Weasel   57

XV A Plain Prose Farewell   63

XVI A Bird of Ill Omen   68

XVII A Homespun Alcalde   70

XVIII Which shows that Tio Lucas is
      a Light Sleeper   73

XIX Voices Crying in the Wilder-
    ness   74

XX Doubt and Certainty   77

XXI	On Guard, My Fine Gentleman!	84
XXII	Weasel Plays Many Parts	90
XXIII	Again the Open Country and Those Voices! ..	93
XXIV	A King of the Old School	94
XXV	The Weasel's Star	97
XXVI	Reaction	99
XXVII	In the King's Name!	100
XXVIII	Ave Maria Purissima!	103
XXIX	The Moon Shines Through the Clouds	106
XXX	A Lady of Quality	108
XXXI	An Eye for an Eye	110
XXXII	Faith Moves Mountains	116
XXXIII	How About Yourself?	119
XXXIV	The Governor's Lady is inviting too	124
XXXV	Imperial Decree	128
XXXVI	Conclusion, Moral and Epilogue	131

INTRODUCTION

The Three-Cornered Hat is an elaboration of a time-honoured Spanish folktale which has been told and re-told a hundred times. Alarcón's version, so spirited, humorous, and richly coloured, was the first to give world currency to the story. Masters of arts other than literature who have made the story the basis of original works have accepted Alarcón's inventions as authentic parts of the legend. Thus the nineteenth-century painter Carbonero illustrated the tale with highly finished studies that interpret excellently the racy and picturesque realism of Alarcón's novel. In the author's own lifetime two operettas, one by a French and the other by a Belgian composer, were made out of it. But the most celebrated of all the works of art founded on the book is, of course, Manuel de Falla's ballet. His music has caused the adventure of the Miller and the Corregidor's Lady to be familiar to thousands who have never heard of Alarcón.

For Alarcón was certainly not one of the big pieces in the artillery of genius made up of great Spanish novelists which bombarded world consciousness in the late nineteenth century. His power fell far short of the serene mastery of Juan Valera, and he could not compare in vigour and knowledge of humanity with Perez Galdos. His taste was notoriously erratic

and even to the end his prose style often curiously
strained and inflated. All but a few of his books—
and the total number is not large—are of minor
merit. Only five or six of his many short tales and
perhaps one other novel seem really worthy of the
hand that wrote *The Three-Cornered Hat*. Alarcón may
fairly be set down as a one-story master, one of an
honoured international company to which belong
the Abbé Prévost, la Motte Fouqué, and our own
R. D. Blackmore, among others. It is a single book
that ensures for each of them a permanent niche in
fame.

The Three-Cornered Hat first appeared in 1874, its
author being forty-one at the time. Before this he had
published nothing very considerable. There was his
sensational firstborn, *The Last Act of Norma* (I use the
title of the English translation of 1891). This is a
novel that to a modern taste seems far-fetched in the
extreme. In addition, he had produced one un-
successful play, one colourful book of war reporting,
two travel books, and a volume of miscellaneous
verse. He had also written a great number of tales,
varied in kind and quality, which he subsequently
collected in several volumes. But before 1874 he had
not made a lasting impression on the public.

Almost at once *The Three-Cornered Hat* was a
resounding success. It has remained so ever since
with readers of Spanish in and beyond its land of
origin. The adroitness of narrative, the rapid and
vivid characterisation, the lively down-to-earth
dialogue, the pervading flavour of robust, mischievous
gaiety, and the profound delight in Spanish life and

things which every page breathes—these qualities deeply impress the reader's imagination and, if he is a foreigner, become part for ever of his mental picture of Spain.

It is a short novel, but then it is in short works that the edge of Alarcón's power is felt keenest. Nearly all his life he was a busy man of affairs and moved in high society; for half of it he was a well-known public figure. Politics, the press, diplomacy, travel, made great demands upon his time. He began as a very young man in political journalism, first in his beloved Guadix, the Granadan town where he was born, and afterwards in Madrid where he edited a radical paper called significantly *The Whip*. As an insistent and outspoken critic of Queen Isabella II he became involved in a duel with a Catholic and Royalist writer who rejoiced in the great name of Quevedo. At the rendezvous Alarcón found himself quite deserted by all his radical friends who at the last minute, perhaps, grew cautious. At any rate, their defection had a disillusioning, as well as a damping, effect upon Alarcón. Quevedo noticed this, and when the duel reached a critical point and Alarcón, novice that he was, had missed with his shot, Quevedo deliberately fired into the air. The contestants then shook hands, honour satisfied. This incident, not unnaturally, started Alarcón's gradual retreat from radicalism and crossing-over into the camp of Rome and traditionalism.

Some years afterwards Spain embarked upon war in Morocco. Alarcón hurried to enlist and in the course of the campaign was wounded. His experiences inspired him to write his *Eye-Witness's Diary of the War in Africa*, published in 1860. This brought him a small fortune and a considerable reputation. He now had the means to make writing tours in Spain, Africa, and Italy, and then launch into an active political career. For years he sat as a deputy in the Cortes, and later served his country abroad as Minister Plenipotentiary to Denmark and Norway.

All the time he went on practising fiction and journalism, but it was naturally short works that most fitted the fragmentary leisure that his busy public life allowed him. *The Three-Cornered Hat* was written in about ten days, and only received its final length and elaboration by a kind of accident. Its author tells us about it in one of his last published writings, *The Story of My Books*. It began as a tale of a few pages intended for a popular monthly magazine in Cuba. A fellow writer and friend heard him read an enlarged second draft of the story and encouraged him to work it up into a complete novel.

Afterwards, Alarcón published several more books, including two novels and two or three collections of his tales. He continued his busy career of miscellaneous literature and journalism till 1887 when an attack of hemiplegia left him half-paralysed. Thenceforth he had to stay at home—a great deprivation for a man who gloried in a brilliant social life. He now rarely saw anybody outside his own family and household, and died near Madrid in 1891.

The testimony of writers who knew him well shows that in private life Alarcón was a charming man, high-spirited, the liveliest of talkers and the warmest

4

of friends. All his life he had a singular delight in writing fiction. '*Oh inefable dicha la de creer seres con la pluma!*' ('Oh happiness beyond words—to create living beings with the pen!')—these words of his, so very characteristic, are strangely affecting. It was in writing about *The Three-Cornered Hat* that Alarcón used them.

H.F.T.

1959

CHRONOLOGICAL NOTES ABOUT
THE AUTHOR

1833 Pedro Antonio de Alarcón y Ariza is born at Guadix in Granada on 10th March.

1847 He begins the practice of law in Granada but soon gives it up.

1853 He makes his first trip to Madrid.

1855 He settles permanently in Madrid, publishes his sensational and preposterous first novel *El Final de Norma*, and edits the firebrand republican review *El Latigo* (*The Whip*).

1857 His play *El Hijo Prodigo* is performed.

1859 He enlists in the army and fights in the campaign in North Africa. He wins the San Fernando Cross for bravery.

1860 His account of his wartime experiences *Diario de un testigo de la guerra en Africa* brings him fame.

1861 He publishes a travel book *De Madrid a Napoles*.

1868 A Liberal Spanish government appoints him Minister Plenipotentiary to Norway and Sweden, but he does not take up the appointment.

1874 In July he publishes *El Sombrero de Tres Picos*.

1875 He publishes *El Escandalo*, a novel advertising his conversion from a liberal radical and republican to a supporter of the Catholic Church.

1877 He is elected to the Spanish Academy.

1880 He publishes another novel *El Nino de la Bola*.

1881 He publishes his short romance *El Capitan Veneno*.

1881-1882 He publishes his tales *Novelas Cortas* in three editions.

1882 He publishes *La Prodiga*, his last novel. Its reception is disappointing. He renounces novel-writing, but continues journalism and other kinds of writing.

1891 He dies on the 10th June at Valdemoro near Madrid.

The Author's Preface

FEW Spaniards, not excluding the least learned or well-read, are unfamiliar with the popular tale on which the present book is based. A rough goatherd, who had never set foot outside the remote hamlet where he was born, was the first whom we ever heard tell it. He was one of those rustic types, quite illiterate but with a natural acumen and gift of comedy, who figure so prominently in our national literature under the name of 'picaros'. Whenever a fiesta was held in the hamlet by reason of a wedding or christening or ceremonial visit by the gentry, it fell to him to be leading jester and mime, to play the buffoon and recite the old ballads and tales. On one such occasion—it was almost a whole lifetime ago or, to be precise, more than thirty-five years—he happened one evening to bemuse and beguile our innocent self (for innocent we were then, in a relative sense) with the verse narrative of *The Corregidor and the Miller's Lady* or, conversely, *The Miller and the Corregidor's Lady*, which we now present to the public under the more transcendental and philosophical title, such as the graver modern taste demands, of *The Three-Cornered Hat*.

We well remember that when the goatherd was in this way so delightfully entertaining us the marriageable lasses present turned several shades pinker—by which sign their fond mamas learned that the story was slightly on the raw side, and started to give the storyteller the rough side of their tongues. But little Repela (that was his name) spoke up boldly for himself, maintaining that there was nothing to be shocked at—his narrative told of nothing that a nun herself or a little girl of four was not well aware of.

'See here now', he contended. 'What is the plain upshot of the story of *The Corregidor and the Miller's Wife*? That a man and his wife lie in the one bed, and that no husband feels easier for another's sleeping with his wife! There's startling news!'

'Hum, that's true enough', the matrons conceded, while the high laughter of their daughters rang in their ears.

'The proof that our friend Repela is in the right'— here the father of the bridegroom broke in—'is that all of us here, grown-ups and children too, are well aware that this very night, as soon as the dancing is over, our Juan and his sweet Manuela are—so to speak—to housewarm that lovely bride-bed which old Gabriela has been showing the girls for them to admire the embroidery on the pillow-cases.'

'And don't forget', said the bride's grandfather, 'in the Book of Scripture itself, and in sermons too, these natural facts are set down for the very children to read, so that they may understand all about the long barrenness of Our Lady Mary, the goodness and chastity of Joseph, and about the trick played by Judith, and—and many other wonderful things which I don't at this moment recall. And so, my friends . . .'

'Never mind! Never mind!' boldly cried the girls. 'Do tell us the story again, Tio Repela—it is so amusing!'

'And, in fact, most edifying!' added grandfather. 'Why, it prompts no one to wickedness, much less teaches any, and none who are wicked in the story go unpunished. . . .'

'Come, begin it again!' the committee of mothers says at last.

So Tio Repela repeats the story; and, his version being judged in the light of the ingenuous criterion just referred to, nobody found anything to demur at —which is as much as to say that he was granted 'due licence to promulgate the same'.

* * *

With the passing of years we have heard many varying versions of that same adventure of the Miller and the Corregidor's Lady, always from the lips of some country-bred wit of the same kidney as the late lamented Repela, and, what is more, we have read it in print in different collections of *The Blind Man's Tales* and even in the famous Ballad of the never-to-be-forgotten Don Agustin Duran.

The crux of the story was always the same—tragi-comical, facetious, fearsomely epigrammatic like all the dramatic moral sermons beloved by the common people; nevertheless, the form, the machinery of incident, the circumstantial development differed a great—a very great—deal from our friend the goatherd's narrative. So much so indeed that Repela would never have recited to a village audience any of the said variations on the theme, not excluding the printed ones, without making every proper young miss stop up her ears in horror and exposing his eyes to the nails of their outraged mothers. So far had the insensitive boors of other provinces exaggerated and distorted the traditional theme which in Repela's classic version issues forth so full of taste, proportion and beauty.

For a long time now we have harboured the plan of reviving the plain truth of the story, of restoring to this rare old tale its original character which was one, there can be no doubt, in which the proprieties met a better fate. And this is not at all surprising. This kind of tale, far from changing for the better, lovelier, and chaster, never circulates among the herd without suffering disfigurement and taint by contact with the vulgar and the makeshift.

So much for the story of the present work. Now let us take the plunge; I mean, of course, make a start on the tale of *The Corregidor and the Miller's Lady*, in the modest hope that your sound judgment, most worthy public, 'after reading it and crossing yourselves more abundantly than if you had seen the Devil' (as Estebanillo Gonzalez says in the opening pages of his book), may deem it a fit and proper matter to be set down in black and white.

CHAPTER I

When it all Happened

It was at the beginning of this long century now past
its maturity. The exact year is not known, but it was
between 1804 and 1808.

Still on the Spanish throne at that time was Charles
IV of the House of Bourbon, 'by the grace of God'—
so ran the coins—and by the oversight, or special
clemency, of Bonaparte—so ran the French des-
patches. All the other European sovereigns who
sprang from Louis XIV had already lost their crowns
(the chief of them his head too) in the violent storm
that swept this ancient corner of the globe after 1789.

Nor was this the only way in which our country
was singular in those days. The Soldier of the Revolution, the son of an obscure Corsican attorney, the
victor of Rivoli, the Pyramids, Marengo, and a
hundred other battles had just assumed the crown of
Charlemagne; he had utterly changed the face of
Europe, creating nations, destroying nations, effacing
frontiers, founding dynasties, transforming in form,
name, position, and even dress the communities
through which he galloped his charger like a human
earthquake, or indeed like that very Antichrist with
whose name and attributes the northern powers
freely invested him. Nevertheless, our forbears—

whom God bless in their innocence—far from hating or fearing him delighted in the contemplation of his amazing exploits just as if these had been the feats of some old hero of chivalric romance or happenings in another planet, with not so much as the merest hint of a suspicion that he would ever dream of coming their way to perpetrate among them the same atrocities he had committed in France, Italy, Germany, and elsewhere. Once a week, or twice at most, the post would arrive from Madrid at the important towns in the Peninsula, bringing a new number of the *Gazette*—not then a daily publication. By this means the leading citizens would learn—if the *Gazette* condescended to bother itself with such details —whether any more battles had been fought with seven or eight kings and emperors as participants, and whether Napoleon was to be found in Milan, Brussels, or Warsaw. For the rest, our fathers went on living in the good old Spanish way at a consummately leisured pace, wedded to their well-seasoned customs in the peace and the grace of God, with their Inquisition and their Friars, their inequality before the Law, their privileges, rights, and exemptions, with absolutely no municipal or political freedom, governed simultaneously by illustrious Bishop and powerful Corregidor (whose powers were indistinguishable, since each was concerned with the temporal as well as with the spiritual), paying tithes, first-fruits, rates, subsidies, levies, loans of all kinds, capitation dues, royal tithes, salt-tax, 'civil fruits', to say nothing of fifty more kinds of tribute the very names of which are now forgotten.

Here ends all that this book has to do with things military and political in that epoch. Our only purpose in mentioning them was to establish that in the year in question—which we shall imagine to be 1805—the Old Order still reigned supreme in Spain in every sphere of public and private life. It was just as if amid so many innovations and upheavals the Pyrenees had been transformed into another Great Wall of China.

CHAPTER II

How they lived in those 'Good Old Days'

IN ANDALUSIA, for instance—the scene of the events about which you are to hear—people of standing went blithely on, rising very early in the morning, going to the Cathedral for Matins—and not only on days of obligation—breakfasting at nine on a fried egg and a cup of chocolate with fingers of buttered toast, lunching between one and two on vegetable stew and an entrée—provided of course they had hunted the day before—otherwise on stew alone, dozing through the afternoon siesta, then taking a stroll in the open air; going off to recite the rosary at their parish church in the gathering dusk; taking more chocolate at the Angelus—this time with biscuits; putting in an appearance, assuming that they really were somebodies, at the reception given by the Governor, the Dean or some other local big-wig; returning home at vespers; shutting the front door before the 'Ave Maria'; dining on salad and a fricasee, that is if fresh anchovies were not forth-coming, and going promptly to bed with their wives —those that had wives at any rate—taking care first, for nine months in the twelve, to have the bed well warmed in advance. . . .

O happy, happy time, when our native land went

sweetly along in quiet and peaceful tenure of all its cobwebs and its dust and its moths, all its observances, beliefs, traditions, uses, abuses, consecrated by the centuries! O happy time wherein society boasted a diversity of classes, of loyalties, of customs! Happy time, I repeat, especially for poets who found round every corner material for interludes, farces, comedies, tragedies, miracles or epics, in place of that prosaic uniformity and flat realism which was spawned by the revolution in France! Happy time indeed!

But enough of dwelling on the past! Enough of generalising and beating about the bush! Now for a resolute plunge into the story of *The Three-Cornered Hat*!

CHAPTER III

A Sprat for a Mackerel

At that time there was near the city of —— a well-known flour mill, long since vanished, situated about a quarter of a league from the town between the foot of a gently sloping hill thick with mazard and cherry trees and a flourishing garden, which served as bank —and sometimes as bed—for the wayward and uncertain river which lords it through the region.

For sundry different reasons this mill had been for a long time past a favourite rendezvous and place of entertainment for the more consequential people of leisure living in the aforesaid city. In the first place, leading to it ran a highway rather less difficult of passage than any of the others thereabouts. Secondly, in front of the mill there was a small stone-paved courtyard, roofed by a vast climbing vine, a roof under which it was good to take the air in summer or to sun oneself in winter by reason of the swaying of the wind-stirred branches. In the third place, the Miller was a man of parts with much discretion and good taste, who possessed what we Spaniards call the 'don de gentes', the gift for people, that is to say the art of making friends and influencing them. He danced attendance on the fine gentlemen who honoured him at his evening gatherings, pressing upon them anything which the season provided such as cherries and mazard, long lettuces unseasoned—which were very good when bread rolls went with them such as their Worships took care to send ahead of themselves—or perhaps melons or grapes, from that same spread of vine which was their canopy, or roasted popcorn in winter-time and roast chestnuts, almonds and walnuts and, now and again on chill evenings, a draught of generous old wine, drunk inside the house, to which at Easter were added a few fritters fried in honey, a cracker, or rusk, or a slice of Alpujarra ham.

I seem to hear the curious reader asking: 'Was the Miller rich then, or was it that his guests had extravagant tastes?' I answer: Neither. The Miller had just a sufficiency, and his gentlemen guests were good taste and dignity personified. But in those days when fifty or more levies were paid to Church and State, a shrewd countryman like our friend was making a sound investment by ingratiating himself as he did with Aldermen, Canons, Friars, Notaries, and other people of consequence. And so there were those who said that Tio Lucas—as our Miller was called—saved a power of money every year by dint of providing general entertainment.

'Your Grace will perhaps let me have an old gate from the house you've just pulled down?' he'd say to one dignitary. And to another: 'Would you, sir, bid them reduce my rates, or sales tax, or civil fruits levy?' 'Your Reverence wouldn't object to letting me pick leaves for my silkworms in the Monastery gardens?' 'Will your Excellency allow me to get a little timber from such-and-such a wood?' 'Please, good Father, write me a chit giving me leave to cut a log or two in the pinewood at So-and-so.' 'All it needs, sir, is your drawing me up a little deed free of charge.' 'This year I cannot pay the polltax. I trust that the suit will go in my favour?' 'Today I came to blows with a fellow and I think he should go to prison for provoking me.' 'Has your Worship by any chance such-and-such a thing that you don't want?' 'Is this or that of any service to you?' 'Can you lend me the mule?' 'Will you be using the carriage to-morrow?' 'May I send for the ass?'

Such were tunes he was always singing, and invariably he got for response a generous and un-selfish '*Como se pide*' or 'As you will'. Which clearly shows that Tio Lucas was not on the road to ruin.

CHAPTER IV

One Glance at a Woman

THE last and perhaps strongest reason which the city
gentry had for visiting Tio Lucas's mill at evening was
that in this way every one of them, clergy and laity
alike, from their lordships the Bishop and the
Corregidor downwards, could gaze their fill at one
of the loveliest and most bewitching creatures ever
to come from the hand of what the Frenchified
writers of that time call 'the Supreme Being'.

The creature in question was named Frasquita—
the Señora Frasquita. At once let me say that the
Señora Frasquita, lawful wife of Tio Lucas, was a
truly virtuous woman and well known to be so by all
the mill's distinguished habitués. What is more,
none ever openly looked at her in the common
manner of a male eyeing a female, or with anything
of sly calculation in his eyes. Her admirers would
express their admiration and even pay court to her
on occasion—always, of course, in her husband's
presence—as a paragon of beauty who did honour
to her Maker and a bewitching piece of femininity
whose innocent high spirits and inoffensive banter
could rejoice the gloomiest spirit. 'She really is a
lovely creature', that virtuous man the Bishop would
say. 'A statue from ancient Greece!' averred a most

learned Doctor of Law and Correspondent of the Academy of History. 'She's a true daughter of Eve!' the Colonel of the Militia boomed. 'A serpent of the Nile, a siren, an arrant witch!' the Corregidor himself contributed. 'For all that a virtuous woman, an angel, a child, a mere four-year-old', was the verdict they all concurred in as, the grapes and nuts lying comfortingly in their stomachs, they jogged back from the mill to their own formal and regimented households.

The 'mere four-year-old' of their common admiration was at that time touching thirty years of age. Her height was not much short of six feet, and she was robust in proportion, perhaps even more so than suited her unusual height. She had none of the statuesque repose suggested by the learned Doctor's simile. She would sway like a reed in the wind, veer like a weathercock, spin around like a top. Her features were more mobile still, even less sculptural. Their liveliness was enhanced by no fewer than five dimples, two in one cheek and one in the other, with a fourth, very tiny, near the left corner of her laughing mouth, and the last and largest nestling in the very middle of her exquisitely rounded chin. Add to all this her constant expression of lurking merriment, the flash in her eye, and the lively tilt of her head as she talked, and you may form some notion of the charm of her looks, so full of spirit and radiance, of health and gaiety.

Neither Señora Frasquita nor Tio Lucas were natives of that region; she came from Navarre, he from Murcia. He had gone to the city of —— at the

age of fifteen as combined page and servant to the
Bishop who then ruled the Church in those parts.
His patron trained him for the Church and, perhaps
with that in view and so that he might not lack for a
'competence', left him the mill as a legacy; but Tio
Lucas, who at the date of his Lordship's death had only
been admitted to minor orders, hung up his cassock
there and then and enlisted for a soldier, having more
a mind to see the world and meet adventures than
say Masses and grind corn. In 1793 he made the
campaign of the Western Pyrenees as orderly to
General Don Ventura Caro of gallant memory, took
part in the assault on Castillo Pinon, and spent a
long time in the northern provinces where he received
in due course a total dispensation from his priestly
vows. He came to know Señora Frasquita in Estella
—she was not, of course, Señora then—and fell in
love with her, married her, and bore her off to
Andalusia to the mill that was fated to be thence-
forward the scene of their pilgrimage through this
'valley of laughter and tears'.

Señora Frasquita, transplanted from Navarre into
this new and lonely life, had never acquired any of
the ways of Andalusia. She remained indeed altogether different from the local ladies, dressing with
more simplicity, naturalness and taste. She washep
more frequently and let the sun and air caress her
bare arms and uncovered throat. She would wear, it
is true, the common feminine dress of the period, the
dress of Goya's women; that is, a skirt half a stride
or, at most, a stride wide, very short, allowing a sight
of her slender feet and something of her well-shaped

legs. She favoured the low round 'décolleté' then fashionable in Madrid, in which city she had stayed for two months with her Lucas while in passage from Navarre to Andalusia. Her hair was all gathered up on top of her head coronet-fashion, revealing the full vivid charm of her head and neck. In each small ear she wore a pendant earring, and more than one handsome ring on the slender fingers of her strong white hands. And then her voice—her voice had all the tones of a musical instrument of widest range, and her laughter was so lighthearted and silvery that it sounded like a peal of Easter Sunday bells.

And Tio Lucas . . .?

CHAPTER V

A Glance all round—and inside—a Man

TÍO LUCAS was uglier than sin itself. He has been so all his life and he was now nearing forty. Nevertheless few such openhearted and genial spirits had ever come from the Creator's hand. Completely captivated by his liveliness, his quickness of mind, and his native wit, the late Bishop had begged him of his parents, who had been shepherds—of real sheep, I mean, not men. On his Lordship's death the boy left the seminary for the barracks and soon was singled out by General Caro to act as his valet and orderly in the field. When at last his military service was over it was just as inevitable that he should take Frasquita's heart by storm as that he should have won the special regard of both Prelate and General. That 'fair maid of Navarre'—who at that date had known a mere twenty springtimes and was the toast of all the young bloods in Estella, many of them young men of fortune—was quite powerless to resist his innumerable social graces, the witty sallies, the quizzing of his little, amorous, simian eyes, the ready smile so full of raillery and mischief, and yet of tenderness too. The young Murcian was indeed so forthcoming, had so much to say for himself, showed constantly such sense, address, spirit and wit, that in the end he completely turned the head not only of the much-sought-after young beauty but of her father and mother as well.

Lucas was in those days, as he still was at the time of our story, of spare build—at any rate, compared with his wife. He had something of a hump on his back, and was very swarthy. He was cleanshaven, his ears were rather long, and his face was pockmarked. On the other hand, his mouth was very well-shaped and his teeth perfect.

It could be said of Lucas that only the shell of the man was rough and ugly; as soon as one got beyond that, his perfections became manifest, and they began with his teeth. Then came the voice, vibrant, flexible, seductive; virile and grave at times; then, when he sought a favour, soft and honeyed—at all times hard to resist. Next there was what that voice said—every single word straight to the point, most apt, ingenious, and persuasive. To sum up, the character of Tio Lucas was a compound of stoutness of heart, staunchness, straightforwardness, commonsense, a readiness to learn, an instinctive or acquired knowledge of many things, a deep contempt for fools whatever their social standing, and a certain spirit of irony, burlesque, and raillery that stamped him in the learned Doctor's eyes as a Quevedo in the raw.

Such, outwardly and inwardly, was Lucas.

CHAPTER VI

A Married Couple's Aptitudes

SEÑORA FRASQUITA loved her Lucas to distraction and counted herself the happiest woman in the world to be adored by him in return. Having no children, they regarded coddling and waiting on each other as the main business of life—not, however, that their mutual attachment was in any way tinged with the sickening, sentimental mawkishness of so many childless couples. On the contrary, they treated each other always with the unaffected good-humour, gaiety, and frankness found in two childhood play-mates who, though having the utmost regard for each other, never speak about, or indeed seem in the least conscious of, their feelings.

Never surely lived a miller better looked after, better turned out, better treated at table, or sur-rounded in his house with more creature comforts, than Tio Lucas. Never was miller's lady, or queen herself, the object of so many attentions, so many little presents and treats as the Señora Frasquita. Never did a mill contain so many things necessary, useful, ornamental, entertaining, and even luxurious as the one serving as stage for our present story.

This happy state of affairs was due in part to the fact that the Señora Frasquita—like the beautiful, lively, buxom daughter of Navarre she was—was ever able, competent, and willing to cook, sew, embroider, sweep, bake, wash, iron, tidy, polish, knead, spin, mend, and darn, as well as sing and dance, play the guitar and the castanets, take a hand at cribbage and 'beat-your-neighbour', and do much more that it would take too long to mention. Another contributory factor was that Tio Lucas was ever able, competent and willing to manage the property, cultivate the land, hunt, fish, be carpenter, smith, mason, help his wife in all the multifarious household tasks, read, write, keep accounts, and much besides.

But all this is to leave unmentioned the rarer side of him—his truly remarkable specialised talents. For instance, Tio Lucas adored flowers, as did his wife, and was so expert in growing them that he had succeeded in producing new species by means of assiduous crossing and grafting. He was by way of being a born engineer and had proved it by constructing a sluice, a syphon-pump, and an aqueduct that had tripled the mill's water supply. He had trained a dog to dance, tamed a snake, and taught a parrot to screech out the hours shown on a sun-dial which the Miller had contrived to make in a party wall. The parrot would thus announce the time with perfect accuracy even on cloudy days and at night.

In conclusion, within the limits of the mill were a kitchen garden yielding every kind of fruit and vegetable; a water-hole enclosed in a kind of arbour of jessamine, in which Tio Lucas and Señora Frasquita would bathe in summer; a flower parterre; a hothouse or winter garden for exotic plants; a drinking-water fountain; two donkeys on which husband and wife used to go to the city or neighbouring villages; a chicken run, a dovecot, an aviary, one hatchery for fish and one for silkworms; beehives whose bees sipped the jessamines round about; a winepress and cellar, on a specially small scale; a kiln, a loom, a forge, a carpenter's shop, and oh! much more, all restricted to an eight-roomed house and little more than three acres of land of the taxable value of ten thousand reals.

CHAPTER VII

The Foundations of Happiness

THEY both indeed loved each other to distraction, did the Miller and his lady. It seemed almost that she was the more in love in spite of her husband's ugliness and her own great beauty. This was because she was inclined to grow jealous and call Lucas to account whenever he was unduly late home from the city or the small towns where he went for grain. Tio Lucas, for his part, actually seemed to delight in the attentions to which the gentry who frequented the mill treated Frasquita. He took a genuine pride and joy in the fact that she was just as attractive to everyone else as she was to himself. Though he knew well enough that in their heart of hearts they had an understandably human desire for her and would have given anything for her to be less chaste, yet he would leave her on her own for whole days together without the least anxiety, never asking questions afterwards about what she had been doing or who had been there in his absence.

The truth was not that Tio Lucas's love was less strong than Frasquita's. It was rather that he had more trust in her faithfulness than she had in his. Moreover, he excelled her in penetration, and knew exactly how far her love for him extended and how much she respected herself. He was, to sum up, a complete man—a man of Shakespearean stamp, of few but intense passions, incapable of doubt, a man whose faith was all or nothing, who either loved or hated to the death, and admitted no comparative degree between total felicity and the utter wreck of happiness. He was, in short, an Othello in homespun, and we meet him now playing his part in what could prove the first act of a tragedy.

Here the reader may ask: 'How come these notes of gloom in so cheerful an overture—these fateful lightnings in so cloudless an atmosphere? Why these premonitions of high drama in such a setting?'

Reader, you shall soon learn.

CHAPTER VIII

The Man in the Three-cornered Hat

IT was two o'clock on an October afternoon.

The Cathedral bell was ringing Vespers—a fact that proclaimed that the midday meal was over for all the leading citizens of Seville.

The Canons were on their way to the Choir and the laity had settled down in their bedrooms for the siesta, particularly those who, like the city officials, for instance, holding office of responsibility, had spent the whole morning at work.

So it was a matter for some comment that at that hour, surely a most unsuitable one for an outing in the country particularly as it was still exceedingly hot, there should set out from the City, on foot and with only one Alguacil in attendance, the Lord Governor of Seville himself. He was a personage easily distinguishable at any time of day or night by the vast span of his three-cornered hat, the gaudiness of his crimson cape, and the peculiar blend of grotesqueness and elegance in his appearance.

Of the cape and the three-cornered hat many still living today could speak, if they would, from first-hand knowledge. I among them, like everyone born in Seville during the last years of Fernando VII's reign, well remembered seeing them, the only decoration traceable on any of the tumbledown walls, hanging by a nail in the ruined tower of his Lordship's former house, the place then having become a playground for his grandchildren. There they hung, those picturesque relics, the black hat on top and the red cape below, a sort of ghostly memento of absolutism, a representation in cloth of the Corregidor or posthumous caricature of his reign done in charcoal and red ochre such as we youthful champions of the 1837 Constitution often drew on those very walls. Yes, there they hung, scaring the birds as once they had scared men, and to this day it makes me a little uneasy to think I should ever have joined in the jeering as the relics went their way through the historic city at carnival time, hoisted high on a chimney sweep's broom or ludicrously perched on the head and shoulders of some waggish popular hero who in this way drew fresh roars of mirth from the rabble. . . . Poor emblem of old authority! To such a level we sank you, we who now would only too gladly summon you back to life!

We have spoken of the grotesque element in the elegance of his Lordship the Corregidor. This lay, it is said, in his being round-backed, even more round-backed than Lucas . . . almost, in a word, a hunchback. He was of less than medium stature, of poor physique and unhealthy appearance, with bow legs and a peculiar gait, or rather a way of swaying back and forth and from side to side which can only be described by saying, fantastic as it sounds, that he seemed lame in both feet. Nevertheless, his features were fine-cut, though he was rather sunken in the cheeks from total lack of teeth. His complexion was olive-brown, like that of most of Castille's children, and he had large, murky eyes in which flashes of choler, cruelty, and self-indulgence would spark momentarily. He had a slender foxy face which bore no stamp of any admirable quality but rather of a spiteful cunning that would stop at nothing, and a self-satisfied air in which the aristocrat and the libertine each showed himself and which hinted that in his far-away youth he had had his way with women in spite of his lame feet and his round back.

Don Eugenio de Zuniga y Ponce de Leon had been born in Madrid of an illustrious family. At this time he was entering his fifty-fifth year and his fourth as Governor, or Corregidor, of the City, where he had married, shortly after his arrival there, the illustrious lady you shall hear more of in due course.

Don Eugenio's stockings, which, apart from his shoes, were the only part of his dress which his very long cape allowed to be seen, were white, and his shoes black with gold buckles. But when the heat in the open countryside obliged him to throw aside his outer covering it could be seen that he wore a fine cambric neckcloth, an undercoat of dove-coloured serge overworked with a pattern of green sprigs and bordered with braid, kneebreeches of black silk, an ample frockcoat of the same material as the under-coat, a rapier with a steel pommel, a tasselled cane, and a pair of gloves or gauntlets, which he was never known to put on, but brandished as a king does his sceptre.

The Alguacil, or Constable, who strode twenty

paces behind his Lordship, was known as Weasel
and certainly lived up to the nickname. Lean, and
extraordinarily lithe, with eyes that seemed to be
everywhere as he walked along, he had a long,
scraggy neck, small, unprepossessing features, and
two bony hands like the stocks of whips. He not only
had the ferret-like look of the born smeller-out of
felons, but seemed in his very person to embody the
rope that was to bind them and the instrument of
their punishment.

The first Corregidor to set eyes on him had
instantly pronounced him his trusted Alguacil. And
Alguacil he had been to no fewer than four suc-
cessive Corregidors.

This Weasel was forty-eight years old, and he too
wore a three-cornered hat, but one much smaller
than his master's. That, I repeat, was of quite
remarkable size. He wore a cape, stockings, and suit
all of black, carried a stick without a tassel, and a spit-
like instrument that served as a sword. With such
dress and insignia the swarthy scarecrow seemed the
very shadow of his fine-feathered master.

CHAPTER IX

Get Along, Neddy!

EVERYWHERE that the great man and his single retainer passed the peasant stopped his work to sweep his cap down to his knees—more from fear than respect, be it said—and, that done, said to his neighbour in an undertone, 'He's off early today, our Lord Corregidor, to see Señora Frasquita!'

'Right early—*and* he goes in private!' And indeed never before had they seen his Lordship make that excursion except in company.

'Hey, Manuel! Why is his Lordship going all in private to see the Navarrese today?' asked one village woman whose husband was leading her along mounted on their ass's crupper. And she tickled the nape of his neck roguishly.

'Don't talk scandal, woman!' the good man replied. 'Señora Frasquita would never . . .'

'Oh, I'm sure of that, but our Corregidor—*he* certainly would. Make love to her, I mean. I've heard say that, of all the folk who have their fun at the mill, the only one with any real mischief in him is that—that petticoat-chaser from Madrid!'

'Petticoat-chaser! Now why do you call him that?' The question was pressed with evident interest.

'I don't speak from my own knowledge. Oh, he'd

take good care, for all that he's Corregidor, not to whisper sweet nothings in my ear!' The speaker happened to be ill-favoured in the extreme.

'Here now, lass, enough of that! I don't believe for a moment Tio Lucas is the man to wink at goings-on like that.'

'That's as maybe. All the same, it's pretty clear that he *does* wink at it', the wife persisted with an obstinate pout.

'Lucas is a proper man', retorted the husband, 'and there's some things a proper man won't bear with!'

'Oh, very well then—you're right! There's an end of it. But if I were Señora Frasquita . . .'

'Get along with you, lass!' the husband cried out —to the donkey this time, deliberately changing the subject. And the little animal broke into a trot and the rest of the dialogue was lost to hearing.

CHAPTER X

From the Trellis

WHILE sallies of this sort passed between the country couples who bowed his Excellency on his way, Señora Frasquita was carefully watering and sweeping the little stone-flagged yard which served as a forecourt to the mill. She set out half-a-dozen chairs in a row under the shadiest part of the vine-trellis. It happened that Lucas had climbed up into this very place and was now cutting off the finest clusters of grapes and arranging them to the best advantage in a wicker basket.

'I tell you, Frasquita', the Miller's voice came floating down from the topmost branches, 'his Lordship is fairly sick with love for you.'

'So I told you myself long ago!' Frasquita retorted. 'Much good may it do him! Have a care now, Lucas! Have a care! You'll fall!'

'Not I! Never fear—I've a firm hold. Yes indeed, that gentleman has taken a great fancy to you!'

'Stale news, I tell you! I know well enough those who fancy me—yes, *and* those who don't! If only I knew why you don't!'

'Because you're so ill-favoured!'

'That I may be, but I could still come and push you down from up there!'

'More likely be eaten alive for your pains.'

'Delightful! And when my fancy men came and saw us they'd say we were like a couple of monkeys!'

'They'd be right too! For you are—a right sweet little monkey. But me a monkey? I look more like a cowled monk with this hump of mine.'

'Which I adore!'

'You will like the Corregidor's much more then—it's bigger than mine!'

'Shame on you, Señor Don Lucas! Don't be so jealous!'

'Me jealous? Of that old humbug? Not a bit. I'm delighted to know he's so smitten with you!'

'Why is that?'

'Because the sin always carries its own penance with it. You need not love him in return, and yet I should be the real Governor of the city all the time!'

'There's vanity! But suppose in the end I did come to love him? Stranger things have happened!'

'That wouldn't worry me overmuch.'

'Why not?'

'Because you wouldn't be yourself then, and not being yourself—or rather the image of you I have in my mind—I shouldn't care a hang if devils from hell ran away with you.'

'No, but truly—what would you do if I were to love him?'

'What would I do? Blessed if I know. As I should then be a different man and not the one I am now I just can't imagine how I should feel.'

'Why would you be a different man?'

Determined to make him answer, Frasquita

stopped her brooming and planted her hands on her hips to stare straight up at him.

Tio Lucas scratched his head as if to dig out some deep-lying notion from inside it; when at length he spoke it was in a graver tone and looking a shade paler than usual.

'I should be a different man because I am at this moment one who believes in you as I believe in my own self, who has no other life than that belief. And therefore—therefore if I lost my belief in you, I should either die or be changed into another man altogether. I should live—exist—in a totally different way. It would be like coming into the world for the first time. Therefore I do not know what I should do to you. Perhaps I should laugh and turn my back on you. Perhaps I should ignore you. Perhaps —but this is a fine game indeed making oneself miserable for nothing! What does it matter to us if all the Corregidors in the world are in love with you? Are you not my own Frasquita?'

'Of course, booby, of course I am your Frasquita. And you are my Lucas, uglier than sin itself, but the cleverest of the clever, with more real goodness in you than a loaf of bread! And loved!—ah, how much loved! When you come down from that trellis you will see! You'd best watch out—I'll pinch and I'll slap—you'll have more nips than you've hairs on your head! Hallo! What's this I see? Here comes my Lord Corregidor—quite unattended. . . . So early too! Something's afoot! . . . It looks as if you were right, Lucas.'

'Mind, now—don't tell him I'm up here in the

vine. The man brings an avowal for you in private, and thinks to steal a march on your humble servant while I'm sleeping out my siesta. It'll be fun hearing him pour out his emotion! Not for worlds would I miss this little confession.' And he deftly handed down the basket to her.

'Don't be so naughty!' she said with a fresh burst of laughter. 'The wicked old Madrileno! Who'd have thought a Corregidor would make a set at little me! But he's coming now—quiet! Oh, look! Weasel was walking behind him, but now he's gone to sit down in the ravine in the shade. What a pantomime! This is going to be more fun than you think!'

And she broke out singing—it was the tune of a local fandango for by now she was as much at home with the Andalusian dances as with those of her native province.

CHAPTER XI

The Bombardment of Pamplona

'GOD keep you, Frasquita!' breathed the Corregidor when, walking on tiptoe, he appeared suddenly under the shady roof of the trellis.

'Why, welcome, my Lord Corregidor!' she replied in the most natural tone, curtseying again and again. 'Your Lordship here at such an hour! And in this heat too! Come, let your Lordship be seated. Here is a nice cool spot. Why didn't your Lordship wait for the other gentlemen? All the chairs are already set out. This evening we are expecting my Lord Bishop in person. He promised my Lucas to come and try the first grapes from the vine. But how is your Lordship? And how is your lady wife?'

The Corregidor's senses swam. The complete privacy in which this interview with Frasquita was taking place made it seem like a dream. Something told him to beware lest unwarily he should fall into some hidden trap.

All he said for answer was: 'Oh, it isn't all that early. . . . It's half-past three . . .'

At that moment the parrot began screeching.

'It's a quarter past two!' Frasquita exclaimed, looking him full in the face. He fell silent like a criminal caught red-handed and unable to say a word for himself.

After a while he asked: 'Lucas, is he asleep?'

It should be said that the Corregidor, like all people without teeth, had a loose and sibilant way of pronouncing words as if he were biting his lips.

'Of course!' replied Frasquita. 'At this time of day he always has a nap wherever he happens to be when the fit takes him—yes, if it were on the edge of a precipice!'

'Well then, let him sleep on!' cried the Corregidor whose face had turned a shade or two paler. 'And you, my dear Frasquita, listen to me. Hark now — come here! Sit down here—by my side! I have many things to say to you, m'dear.'

'I am sitting down,' Frasquita replied, clutching a low chair and planting it in front of the Corregidor and very close to his. Once seated, Frasquita threw one leg across the other, leaned forward, propped an elbow on the knee that was uppermost, and cradled her lovely, blooming face in one hand. In this posture, her head tilted slightly, a smile on her lips, all five dimples in play, and her serene eyes fixed on the Corregidor, she waited for him to speak. An observer might have been reminded of the city of Pamplona awaiting the bombardment.

The poor man made to speak, then stopped short, open-mouthed, spellbound by her supreme loveliness, her dazzling charm, and he told himself that this truly wonderful woman, with her alabaster colouring, her gorgeous figure, her radiantly smiling mouth, and her blue unfathomable eyes, could well have been a creation of Rubens.

'Frasquita!' after a long moment he murmured weakly, all the while showing on his withered features, where beads of sweat formed and dropped onto his hunched shoulders, an intense agony. '. . . Frasquita!'

'You repeat my name', Frasquita said. 'What is it?'

'The favour you are asking . . .', began the old man in a tone of infinite tenderness.

'The favour I am asking', said Frasquita, 'your Lordship already knows well what it is. It is that you nominate as Secretary to the City Corporation a nephew of mine in Estella . . . who can then leave that backwater where he has to do without so many of the good things he ought to have. . . .'

'I told you, Frasquita, that is impossible. The present Secretary—'

'—is a thief, a drunkard, and a fool!'

'I know. . . . But he has good backing among the Life Aldermen and I cannot nominate anyone else without the approval of the Corporation. If I do, I run the risk . . .'

'Risk! Risk! What risk would *we* not run for your Lordship?—all of us in this house down to the very cats!'

'Do you really think so much of me?' said his Lordship broken-voiced.

'No, indeed, sir. Thinking anything of your Lordship is a waste of time.'

'Woman, don't lordship me! Speak to me as an

equal—as you would like. Tell me what you wish of me. Do!'

'Am I not telling you what I wish?'

'But . . .'

'No buts now! Bear in mind what a fine worthy young man my nephew is!'

'Well, *you*, dearest Frasquita, are certainly a fine worthy woman!'

'You like me well enough?'

'Like you well enough? You're a woman above all your sex.'

'Look!—there's nothing false about this.' And she rolled up the sleeve of her blouse and showed the Corregidor the rest of her arm, which could have been a caryatid's and was whiter than a lily.

'Like you well enough!' The Corregidor repeated with feeling. 'Night and day at all hours and in all places my thoughts are only of you!'

'So! You do not care then for your lady wife!' Frasquita's pretence of sympathy for the noble lady was so forced it would have made a dying man laugh. 'How sad! My Lucas told me he had had the happiness of speaking to her when he went to mend the clock in your bedchamber, and she was very beautiful and kind, with the sweetest disposition!'

'An exaggeration!' muttered the Corregidor rather sourly.

'On the other hand, others have told me', Frasquita went on, 'that she has a very bad temper and you fear her like the devil. . . .'

'Another exaggeration!' growled the Corregidor, the blood rushing to his face. 'Both stories are

45

exaggerations! The lady has her little whims, certainly, but it's a far cry from that to making me afraid. I am the Corregidor!'

'Yes, but do you love her, or do you not?'

'Well, now . . . I love her a great deal, or rather used to love her before I knew you. But ever since I saw you I don't know what has come into me. She *too* knows something's amiss. It's enough that now touching my wife's face means no more to me than touching my own. D'you see? All my love and feeling for her has vanished. Whereas to touch *your* hand, *your* arm, *your* cheek, *your* waist, I'd give all I have and more!'

As he spoke the Corregidor tried to grasp the bared arm which Frasquita paraded before his eyes. She, however, without the slightest loss of composure, stretched forward and touched his Lordship's chest with a hand as calmly firm and irresistible as an elephant's trunk, and pushed him over backwards, chair and all.

'*Ave María Purísima!*' she cried and laughed uncontrollably. 'The chair must have been broken!'

'What's happening below there?' From over their heads Tío Lucas suddenly thrust his homely face between two clusters in the ceiling of the vine-trellis. The Corregidor meanwhile lay on the ground, staring up in strange alarm at the other man. At that moment he could have served as model for the Devil overthrown by—I won't say St Michael but another creature from Hell.

'What's happening?' Frasquita quickly took up

46

Lucas's words. 'Why, my Lord Corregidor tipped his chair too far back, overbalanced, and fell!'

'*Jesús, María y José!*' exclaimed the Miller. 'Has your Lordship hurt yourself? Would you like a little water and vinegar?'

'There are no bones broken!' said the Corregidor, scrambling to his feet as best he could. And he added in a tone that Frasquita was able to hear, 'You'll pay for this!'

'Your Lordship saved my life!' Tío Lucas said, not budging from his position on top of the trellis. 'Just fancy, wife! I was sitting up here admiring the grapes when I dropped off to sleep on a network of vine shoots and sticks with gaps between as big as my body. So if his Lordship's tumble hadn't woken me in the nick of time I should have fallen and broken my head on those flags down there.'

'Is that so, eh?' said the Corregidor. 'Then, bless me, I'm glad of it. I declare I'm glad I took a tumble! . . . You'll pay me for this!' The last sentence was in an undertone for Frasquita's ear. It was given with a look of such concentrated fury that Frasquita felt uneasy. She could clearly see that the Corregidor had been apprehensive at first that the Miller had heard everything. But now, reassured that he had heard nothing—for the naturalness with which Lucas acted his part would have taken in the shrewdest eye—he was beginning to give a free run to his fury and think of ways of revenge.

'Here! Come down from there and help me brush down his Lordship! He's smothered in dust.'

As Lucas climbed down she flicked at the Corregidor's coat with her apron and whispered in his ear, 'The poor man heard nothing. He was sleeping like a log.' Even more than her actual words the fact that she spoke them in an undertone—an open assumption of collusion between them—had an almost magical effect upon him. 'You sly thing! You naughty girl!' he babbled, his mouth watering, while he still outwardly assumed a grumbling tone.

'Your Lordship won't bear me any malice?' Frasquita pleaded.

Severity appeared to be yielding such good results that the Corregidor made to give Frasquita a look of anger, but, meeting her disarming smile and the irresistible appeal of her divine eyes, he said in a small, tenderly caressing voice: 'That rests with you, my love!'

Then Tio Lucas dropped down from the trellis.

CHAPTER XII

Tithes and First Fruits

ONCE the Corregidor was in his seat again, Frasquita shot a quick glance at her husband and saw him as self-possessed as ever, though secretly bursting with a desire to laugh at what was passing. She blew him a kiss the first time his Lordship's eye was averted, then, in a siren voice that might have made Cleopatra jealous, said, 'Now your Lordship must try my grapes'.

What a picture she made, the lovely Frasquita then! Were I a Titian I should have painted her in just such a posture—poised in front of the utterly enthralled Corregidor, vivid, alluring, magnificent, her tall, splendid figure in its close-fitting dress, her bare arms arched above her head with a glowing bunch of grapes dangling from each hand. So standing, she turned on the old man a smile that, while utterly enchanting, was still a little pleading, a little fearful, and added : 'They haven't yet been tried by my Lord Bishop. They're the first we've had this year. . . .' Doubtless she would have reminded the learned Doctor of the tall figure of Pomona, offering fruits to some rustic god or satyr.

Just then, right at the end of the little flagged court-

49

yard came into view the reverend Bishop of the diocese, with the learned Doctor himself and two elderly canons. The Bishop paused a moment to take in the scene before him, so comical and yet so charming; then, using the quiet, gentle tones of the typical prelate of his day, he said: 'Fifthly, pay tithes and first fruits to the Church of God. Thus Christian doctrine teaches us. You, however, my Lord Corregidor, not content with administering the tithe, make it also your business to devour the first fruits.'

'The Lord Bishop!' Both the Miller and his wife cried and ran from the Corregidor's side to kiss the prelate's ring. 'May God reward your Lordship for coming to honour this humble house!' said Tio Lucas, kissing the ring first, in a tone of the deepest reverence. 'How fine and well my Lord Bishop looks!' cried Frasquita, kissing the ring after her husband. 'God bless and keep him more years than he has kept my own Lucas!'

'I can't see what use I am here since you bestow blessings instead of asking them', remarked the priest, smiling good-humouredly. Extending two fingers, he blessed first Frasquita, then the others standing around her.

'Here, your Lordship, are the first fruits.' The Corregidor took a bunch from Frasquita's hand and offered it ceremoniously to the Bishop. 'I haven't yet tasted the grapes', he added with an ironical glance towards Frasquita.

'But not because they are green like those in the fable', observed our learned lawyer.

'Those in the fable', the Bishop gently corrected,

'weren't green, Master Licentiate, but out of the fox's reach.'

Neither had intended any allusion to the Corregidor, but the remarks of both fitted recent happenings so aptly that the Corregidor turned crimson with anger and remarked as he bent over the Bishop's ring.

'That's as much as to call me a fox, reverend sir!'

'*Tu dixisti*', retorted the Bishop with the mild insistence of a true saint. '*Excusatio non petita, accusatio manifesta. Qualis vir, talis oratio. Pero satis jam dictus. Nullus ultra sit sermo.* Or, what amounts to the same thing, let us give over Latin and take a look at these precious grapes.' And he plucked a single grape from the bunch which the Corregidor was holding out. 'Indeed they're very fine!' he pronounced, holding the grape up against the light and then handing it behind to his Secretary. 'A great pity they don't agree with me.' The Secretary in his turn surveyed the grape critically, made a polite gesture of approval, and passed it on to one of the retinue who aped both the Bishop's action and the Secretary's gesture, even going so far as to take it up to his nostrils, and then . . . lay it in the basket with scrupulous care, remarking to the bystanders in a whisper, 'His Lordship is fasting'. Tio Lucas, whose little eyes had closely followed every stage of the grape's progress, at once plucked it out and devoured it unobserved.

After this the whole company sat down, and talk went round—talk, for instance, of the weather that autumn—for it was persisting very dry in spite of the first October storm having come and gone; then there was some discussion of the prospect of a new war between Napoleon and Austria, and everyone was emphatic that the Emperor's troops would never invade Spanish territory. The learned Doctor shook his head over the topsy-turvy and calamitous nature of the times, lamenting the peaceful days of his forbears, just as his forbears had lamented those of theirs. Five o'clock was screeched by the parrot, and at a sign from the reverend Bishop, the very smallest of the pages went off to the episcopal coach (which stood in the same ravine where Weasel sat waiting) and brought back a delicious seed cake powdered with salt scarcely an hour out of the oven. A little table was then set up in the midst of the company, and the cake was cut into four pieces of which Tio Lucas and Frasquita, after first modestly declining with great firmness, were persuaded to take a share. And a truly democratic equality reigned for a full half-hour underneath vine-clusters tenderly coloured by the glow of the setting sun.

CHAPTER XIII

Said the Jackdaw to the Raven

AN HOUR and a half later all the distinguished
picnickers were back in the city.

My Lord Bishop and his household had arrived
with due punctuality, thanks to the coach, and were
already in the palace where we will leave them
saying their devotions.

The eminent lawyer, who was very learned, and
the two canons, perfectly matched in corpulence and
respectability, went on with the Governor as far
as the town hall where his Excellency said he had
work to do, and then made their way towards their
respective houses. They found their way, like
mariners, by the stars, and groped their way round
corners like blind men, for night had already closed
down on the city. The moon was not yet out, and all
public lighting, like this present age's own luminaries,
existed only in the mind of the Creator.

All the same it was common enough to meet at
that time, proceeding through one or other of the
city streets, a lantern or link with which the obse-
quious lackey lighted his splendid lord or lady on
their way to a nightly entertainment or a visit to
some kinsfolk.

Up against most of the low railings could be detected (more by the nose than the eye, if truth be told) certain dark shadowy silent forms. These were gallants who, hearing footsteps, had paused a moment in the conduct of their amours.

The lawyer and the two canons were meanwhile passing the journey away with the following exchanges.

'What macaronies we are! Whatever will they think at home when they see us come in at such an hour?'

'What will passers-by in the street think meeting us at something past seven of night hugging the shadows like bandits?'

'We must mend our ways.'

'Indeed we must! But oh! that divine mill!'

'My wife can't abide the mention of it', said the lawyer—in a tone which betrayed considerable apprehension of the approaching conjugal reunion.

'And as for my niece', put in one of the canons—he must certainly have belonged to a penitentiary order —'my niece says clerics shouldn't pay calls on lady friends.'

'And yet', put in his companion who belonged to a preaching order, 'all that goes on in the mill is as innocent as can be.'

'Of course! Doesn't my Lord Bishop go there himself?'

'But then, gentlemen, at our age!' objected the penitentiary. 'Yesterday I reached my five-and-seventieth year.'

'Evidently!' replied the preacher. 'But let's talk

of other things. How lovely Señora Frasquita was tonight!'

'As to that, she was lovely enough, certainly', said the lawyer with a show of disinterestedness.

'Very lovely!' re-echoed the penitentiary from amid his wrappings.

'If anyone doubt it', added the preacher, 'ask the Corregidor. . . .'

'The poor man is quite in love with her!'

'You're right!' exclaimed the confessor.

'Most assuredly!' added the lawyer. 'Well, gentlemen, I'm taking a short cut home from here. A very goodnight to you both!'

'Goodnight', answered the canons. They went on a few paces in silence.

'*He's* sweet on the miller's lovely wife, too!' muttered the preacher, giving his brother, the penitentiary, a nudge.

'So it would seem!' the other replied, stopping at the door of his house. 'But what a churl he is! Well, till tomorrow, friend. I hope the grapes agree with you.'

'Till tomorrow, if God will. . . . May you have a good night.'

'God give us both good nights!' said the penitentiary piously from his porch where could be seen a lamp and a figure of the Virgin.

And he gave a rap with the knocker.

Left alone in the street, the other canon, who was as broad as high and seemed to roll in his gait, passed on in the direction of his house. Before reaching it, however, he stepped aside to a wall, committing an act which years later was to come under a police ban as a misdemeanour. At the same time he muttered to himself, thinking no doubt of his colleague in the choir.

'And you're sweet on Señora Frasquita yourself!' adding a second later, 'And, as lovely goes, she certainly is lovely!'

CHAPTER XIV

Advice from The Weasel

MEANWHILE the Corregidor had climbed up the stairs
of the town hall with Weasel in close attendance.
With the latter he kept up for some time in the
assembly room a conversation of a more familiar
kind than was proper for one of his rank and quality.

'My Lord, take the word of an old game dog who
knows the hunt!' the rascally bailiff was saying.
'Señora Frasquita is desperately in love with your
Worship and all that your Worship has been telling
me only makes it clearer to me, as clear as that lamp
yonder. . . .'

He pointed to a brass lamp which lit up a bare
eighth of the room.

'I am not so sure, Weasel', replied Don Eugenio,
sighing forlornly.

'But why not? But say that she weren't now—let's
be quite frank. Your Worship—pardon me for
saying so—has a bodily defect, is it not so?'

'I have indeed!' agreed the Corregidor. 'But that
defect—why, Tio Lucas has it too. He has more of a
stoop than I have!'

'Much more! Very much more! There's no com-
parison whatever! But on the other hand—and here
is my point—Your Worship has a right well-favoured

countenance . . . it could indeed be called a handsome countenance. Whereas Tío Lucas looks like Sergeant Utrera, fairly brimming over with ugliness.'

The Corregidor smiled with pleased vanity.

'And what's more', the Bailiff added, 'Señora Frasquita would willingly throw herself out of a high window if she could thereby secure the appointment of her nephew . . .'

'Ah, there I'm with you! That appointment is my only hope!'

'Well, to business, sir! I have explained to your Worship my own plan. It rests only to put it into action this very night.'

'I've told you many a time I don't want your advice!' Don Eugenio shouted, recollecting suddenly that he was talking with an inferior.

'I thought you had asked for . . .', Weasel began stammering.

'Don't answer me back!'

The Weasel bowed.

'Well now, you were saying', resumed Don Eugenio, calming down again, 'that this very night I can settle this whole matter? Look you, man, that contents me very well. Why, the Devil! that would soon free me from this cruel uncertainty!'

Weasel made no comment.

The Corregidor went to the writing-table and wrote a few lines on a sheet of paper with a seal attached. He affixed his own seal mark and stowed the document in his pocket.

'Now it's done—her nephew's appointment!' he

announced, taking a pinch of snuff. 'Tomorrow I'll settle with the Aldermen, and either they ratify it or there'll be a massacre! Don't you think that's the way?'

'That's it! That's it!' cried Weasel, full of enthusiasm, putting a lean paw in the Corregidor's snuffbox and taking a pinch. 'That's the very thing! Your Worship's predecessor likewise never let things stand in his way!'

'Stop your prattling!' broke in the Corregidor, delivering a sharp flick on the other's pilfering hand.

'My predecessor was a dolt when he had you for his Alguacil. But let's return to things of importance. You tell me Tio Lucas's mill is situated in the limits of the adjoining district, and not of this town. Are you sure of that?'

'Very sure! The jurisdiction of the City ends at the little ravine where I sat this evening waiting while your Excellency . . . I vow to Lucifer! If I had been in your Lordship's shoes. . . !'

'Enough!' growled Don Eugenio. 'You are insolent!'

Seeing a half-sheet of paper, he wrote a note, folded it, turned up a corner and handed it to Weasel. 'Here', he said as he did so, 'is the letter you sought for the Alcalde of the district in question. You will explain verbally all he has to do. You observe that I follow your plan to the letter. Woe to you if you lead me into a cul-de-sac!'

'Have no fear of that!' answered Weasel. 'Señor Juan Lopez has much to fear, and as soon as he sees your Lordship's signature he will do all I tell him.

He owes at least a thousand fanegas of corn to the Royal Granary and as much again to the Church Granary! This last debt is quite illegal since he's no poor widow or labouring man entitled to receive wheat without interest or charges, but a gambler, a drunkard, a man without shame, a great wencher who has scandalised his whole district! And that man exercises authority! But that's the way of the world!'

'I told you to hold your tongue! You're distracting me!' shouted the Corregidor. 'Now let's get to business', he soon added in a changed tone. 'It's a quarter past seven. . . . The first thing you have to do is to go to the house and tell her ladyship not to expect me to dinner or to bed either. Tell her that tonight I shall be at work right up to the curfew hour, and after that I shall be going forth with you on a secret watch to apprehend certain malefactors. At any rate, see that your story is good enough to send her to bed without a doubt in the world! On the way back, tell the other bailiff to bring my supper . . . I dare not face her ladyship tonight. She knows me so well that she could read my very thoughts. Charge the cook to set out some of the honey fritters she made today, and tell young Juan to go to the tavern and fetch me half a pint of white wine. And to be sure that nobody sees him. Then off with you directly to the village, which you should reach at half-past eight.'

'I'll be there at eight sharp!' Weasel cried.

'Don't contradict me!' roared the Corregidor, again remembering his dignity.

Weasel bowed.

'We said', the other went on, his tone again good-tempered, 'that at eight sharp you'll be at the village. From the village it will be—hm, I think it will be half a league.'

'A short one.'

'Don't interrupt me!'

The Weasel bowed again.

'A short one', went on the Corregidor. 'So there-fore . . . do you think that by ten o'clock . . . ?'

'Before ten o'clock! At half past ten your Worship can knock on the door of the mill with perfect security!'

'What's this! Don't tell me what I have to do! Now then—you will be . . . ?'

'I shall be everywhere. . . . But my usual post will be the little ravine. Ah, I nearly forgot! Your Worship should go on foot and carry no lantern. . . .'

'The devil a need there is for all this advice! Do you think this is the first time I've had an out-of-town adventure?'

'I'm sorry, your Worship. . . . Ah, another thing. Don't knock at the great door opening on to the stone courtyard but at the little door which is over the millstream . . .'

'Over the millstream? Is there another door there? Why, that's something I've never noticed myself!'

'Yes, sir, the little millstream door leads right to the sleeping quarters of the Miller and his lady . . . and Tio Lucas never goes in or out by that door. So that, even if he did come back sooner than expected. . . .'

'I see, I see. . . . Don't keep dinning things in my ear!'

'One last thing! Be sure your Worship flits away before sunrise. That at present happens at six. . . . '

'Another needless piece of advice! At five I shall be back in my own house. . . . But we have talked enough! Out of my sight now!'

'Well then, sir—good fortune to your Worship!' exclaimed the Alguacil, at the same time extending the palm of his hand sideways while he gazed up at the ceiling.

The Corregidor dropped a peseta in the hand and Weasel vanished as if by magic.

'By ——!' muttered the Corregidor after a moment. 'I forgot to tell that windbag to have them bring me a pack of cards! It would have helped me while away the time till half-past nine, seeing whether I could play out a game of solitaire . . . !'

CHAPTER XV

A Plain Prose Farewell

IT WAS about nine o'clock that night when Tio Lucas and Señora Frasquita, all the chores of mill and household finished, ate a supper of meat fried with tomatoes, and a few of the grapes that were left in the famous basket, washed down with a little wine and a great deal of laughter at the Corregidor's expense. Then the couple looked long at each other across the table like people well content with God and themselves. A kiss passed between them, then one said, 'Come, let's go up to bed. Tomorrow will be another day.'

Just then two heavy, insistent knocks sounded on the outer door of the mill. Husband and wife eyed each other in alarm. Never before had anyone knocked at their door at such an hour.

'I'll go and see . . .' the stout-hearted Frasquita began, taking a step towards the courtyard.

'Stay where you are! This is my affair!' Lucas spoke with such authority that Frasquita at once obeyed. 'I said you were not to go out', he added sharply as the obstinate woman was about to follow him. Obediently she stayed where she was.

'Who is it?' Tio Lucas demanded from the middle of the courtyard.

'The Law!' a voice from the other side of the door answered.

'What law?'

'The Law of the district. Open in the name of the Señor Alcalde!'

'You mean "Open in the name of that drunkard the Alcalde"!' said the Miller drawing back the bolt.

'The same!' the voice answered. 'I bring a written summons from his Worship. A very good evening to you, Tio Lucas. . . .' This greeting was added by Tonuelo as he came through the open door, his tone now less officious, gruff, and pompous, almost a different man's.

'God keep you, Tonuelo!' said the Miller. 'Let's see the summons you have there. Master Juan Lopez might have picked a different and more suitable time for calling on respectable citizens! But, of course, you're to blame! It's plain to see you've been tippling in all the little farmhouses on the road here. Would you like a glass of something?'

'No, señor. There's no time for a glass of anything. You must come with me at once. Read the summons!'

'Come with you, eh?' Tio Lucas took the paper from him and turned into the house. 'Let me look. Frasquita, give us a light!'

Frasquita put down something she was holding and took an oil lamp down from its hook. The Miller caught a glimpse of the object his wife had dropped and recognised the trumpet-mouth of his huge blunderbuss which loaded bullets of half a pound weight or more. He gave her a look full of tender appreciation and took her face in his hands. 'What

64

a woman you are!' Frasquita, pale but cool as a marble statue, held up the lamp in her two fingers, her wrist perfectly steady, and, very matter-of-fact, she said, 'Read it then.'

The summons ran: 'For the better service of His Majesty the King, our Liege Lord, (whom God preserve), I warn Lucas Fernandez, Miller of these parts, that as soon as he receives the present summons he shall appear before my Worship offering no excuse whatever; and I direct him that by reason of the matter's being most confidential he communicate it to no man; and all this on pain of the customary forfeits in the event of disobedience.'

The summons ended: 'The Alcalde—Juan Lopez.' And there was a cross instead of a seal.

'Now see here—what on earth does this summons mean?' Tio Lucas asked the Alguacil.

'I don't know', Tonuelo answered. He was a thorough countryman, about thirty years old, with sharp, irregular features that suggested the thief and cutthroat and were the worst possible recommendation. 'I think it's a kind of enquiry into some witchcraft or coining. You are being called as an expert witness. But, to be sure, I don't know about the details. Master Juan Lopez will explain it more fully.'

'Very well, then', said the Miller. 'Tell him I'll come tomorrow.'

'No! No, Master! You are to come right now without a moment's delay! That is the order given me by Master Alcalde.'

There was a moment of silence. Fire seemed to dart from Frasquita's eyes. Tio Lucas kept his on the

65

ground as if searching for something. 'You will grant me, at any rate, 'he said at last, 'time to go to the stable and saddle an ass. . . .'

'The devil I will!' Tonuelo shook his head. 'Anyone can do a half-league journey on foot! The night's a fair one, there's a moon, and——'

'I noticed it had risen. But my feet are all swollen up——'

'Then lose no time! I'll help you saddle the beast.'

'So, you're afraid I'll run away?'

'I'm afraid of nothing, Tio Lucas', answered Tonuelo with a brazenly cool look. 'I am the Law.' He rested his arms on his hips, allowing through the gaping ends of his shaggy cape a glimpse of the fowling-piece he carried under it.

'Tonuelo', said Frasquita. 'Seeing that you are going to the stable—in the performance of your legal duty—will you be good enough to saddle the other ass as well?'

'For whom?' asked her husband.

'For myself ! I'm going with you.'

'Out of the question, Señora Frasquita!' Tonuelo made a short, vigorous gesture. 'My orders were to fetch your husband—nothing more. And to prevent you from coming after us. My very neck depends upon it! In those very terms I was charged by Master Juan Lopez. Come, let's be off, Tio Lucas!' He moved towards the door.

'This is a mighty queer business', muttered the Miller, not attempting to follow for the moment.

'Very!' agreed Frasquita.

'There's something behind this—of that I'm sure

. . . ' Tio Lucas went on muttering to himself in a tone that Tonuelo could not hear.

'Do you want me to go to the city', whispered Frasquita, 'and inform the Corregidor what is happening?'

'No!' Tio Lucas's voice rose. 'Don't do that!'

'Then what *do* you want me to do?' insisted Frasquita.

'Do? Look at me!' His voice and look reminded her that he had once been a soldier. Their eyes held each other in silence a while and they drew so much reassurance from the calm steadfastness and strength which their hearts communicated to each other that in the end their shoulders began shaking and they burst out laughing.

Then Tio Lucas lit another light and made off for the stable, ironically flinging at Tonuelo as he brushed past him: 'Come on, man! Come and help me—if you'll be so good!' Tonuelo turned after him, whistling a tune between his teeth.

A few minutes later Tio Lucas set off, mounted on a fine she-ass, with Tonuelo bringing up the rear. The farewell exchanges of husband and wife were of the briefest.

Tio Lucas: 'Lock up securely now!'

Frasquita, making good use of key, bolt, and bar: 'Keep yourself wrapped up—it's chilly weather!'

No word more of goodbye, not a kiss, embrace, or even a look, for none was needed.

CHAPTER XVI

A Bird of Ill Omen

LET US too go along with Tio Lucas.

They had travelled nearly a mile without a single word, the Miller on the ass and the Alguacil urging it on with his staff of office, when they sighted ahead of them, at the crest of a rise in the road, a shadow like that of a huge bird advancing upon them.

This shadow stood out sharply against the sky, lit up by the moonlight which outlined it with such brilliant clarity that the Miller at once exclaimed:

'Tonuelo, that's Weasel with his three-cornered hat and wiry legs!'

Before the other could reply the shadow, anxious no doubt, to avoid meeting them, swerved away from the road and began rapidly travelling across country as if it had been a weasel in reality.

'I can't see anybody.' After a long pause Tonuelo's answer was spoken with the most natural air in the world.

'Neither can I', replied Tio Lucas.

And the suspicion which had sprung to his distrustful mind in the mill began to take definite form.

'This little journey of mine', he told himself, 'is a love ruse of the Corregidor's. The avowal I heard this afternoon from the top of the trellis proves the old dodderer can't wait any longer. Doubtless he is paying a return visit to the mill tonight, and with that in view has begun by getting me out of the way. However, what of it? Frasquita is Frasquita! She won't open that door—not if they set fire to the house, she won't! No indeed, and, what's more, even if she did, even if the Corregidor succeeded in taking my good lass in by some trick or other, the old rascal'd only come out of it all with a flea in his ear! Frasquita is Frasquita! For all that', he added a moment later, 'I'd better be back home tonight as soon as I can!'

At this point they arrived at the village and made for the house of his worship the Alcalde.

CHAPTER XVII

A Homespun Alcalde

THE WORTHY Juan Lopez, who both in his private character and his public office was tyranny, ferocity, and pride personified when he had to do with his inferiors, was nevertheless pleased at that hour, having finished official business and matters relating to his farm, and administered the daily hiding to his wife, to drink a *cantaro* of wine in company with the Secretary and the Sacristan. This activity had already been proceeding for half the night when the Miller made his appearance in the company.

'Hallo, Tio Lucas', said Master Lopez, giving his head a scratch to stimulate its inventiveness. 'And how are you? Secretary, pour a glass of wine for Tio Lucas! And Señora Frasquita? Is she as lovely as ever? It's such a long time since I saw her! Gad, though! How excellently the corn is ground now-adays! Ryebread tastes like best quality wheaten! Well, now! Sit you down and rest yourself! Luckily, there's no hurry!'

'Hurry!' Lucas repeated the word. 'To the devil with hurry!' His suspicions increased inwardly every moment as he saw the friendly reception which was being given him, following upon so stern and in-sistent a summons.

'Well then, Tio Lucas', the Alcalde went on, 'you are obviously in no great hurry yourself. You'll sleep here tonight and tomorrow early we'll settle your little affair. . . .'

'That will suit me', agreed Tio Lucas, ready to meet Master Juan's dissimulation with his own. 'Providing the business is not pressing . . . I'll spend the night away from home.'

'Neither pressing nor in any way prejudicial to you, my friend', continued the Alcalde, himself taken in by his intended dupe. 'You can set your mind perfectly at rest. Listen, Tonuelo. Push out that half fanega keg for Tio Lucas to sit on.'

'All right then!' said the Miller, sitting down. 'Give me another drink!'

'Here you are!' said the Alcalde, handing him a glass full to the brim.

Tio Lucas made the customary polite acknowledgement. 'It's in good hands. . . . Try a half yourself !'

'Your health, then!' said Master Juan Lopez, drinking a half of the wine.

'And yours, Master Alcalde!' answered Tio Lucas, drinking off the other half.

'Here, Manuela', the Alcalde called. 'Tell your mistress that Tio Lucas is staying the night here. Let her put a pillow in the loft. . . .'

'Gad, no! I'll not hear of it! I'm sleeping in the barn—like a king!'

'See now, we've plenty of pillows . . .'

'I know you have! But why put the whole household out? I'm wearing my capote!'

'Very well, my dear sir, as you will! Manuela, tell your mistress she need not——'

'One favour I would ask', put in Tio Lucas with a tremendous yawn. 'And that is—let me go to bed directly. I did a deal of grinding yesterday and I haven't yet had a wink of sleep.'

'Granted!' the Alcalde said royally. 'You may go to bed whenever you like.'

'I think it's time we went, too', said the Sacristan, eyeing the wine flask in an effort to calculate what remained inside. 'It must be ten o'clock—or not much short.'

'A quarter to ten', announced the Secretary after sharing out in the glasses the rest of the night's wine allowance.

'To bed then, gentlemen', cried their host, tossing off his share.

'Till tomorrow, my masters!' put in the Miller, drinking his.

'Wait till they bring you a light. Tonuelo, take Tio Lucas to the barn.'

'This way, Tio Lucas!' said Tonuelo, lifting up the flask in case a few drops were left.

'Till tomorrow if God will—' added the Sacristan, after draining every glass, and off he staggered humming the *De Profundis*.

'Well, friend', the Alcalde said to the Secretary when they were alone. 'Tio Lucas suspects nothing. We can go to bed now with easy minds. Much good may it do the Corregidor!'

CHAPTER XVIII

Which shows that Tio Lucas is a Light Sleeper

FIVE minutes later a man quietly let himself down from the window of the Alcalde's barn which looked out on a large yard and was less than four feet from the ground.

In the yard stood a shed housing a great stable in which six or seven mounts of mixed breed, all mares, were tethered. Stallions, mules, and donkeys occupied a separate hut next door. The man untied an ass which stood ready saddled, and, leading it by the halter, made for the yard gate. He drew back the bolt and undid the latch which fastened it. He opened the gate forthwith and found himself in an open field.

Once there, he mounted the ass, applied his heels to its flanks, and shot off straight as an arrow in the direction of the city—not, however, by the usual track but across ploughed fields and down cattle paths as though he was anxious to avoid unwelcome encounters.

The man was, of course, Tio Lucas.

CHAPTER XIX

Voices Crying in the Wilderness

'WHAT! Alcaldes on my track, and me, a man from Archena!' Lucas kept saying to himself, proudly remembering his Murcian birthplace, as he rode on. 'Tomorrow morning I'll go and see the Lord Bishop and tell him all that has happened to me this night. To send me such an urgent summons at such an unearthly hour, tell me to come alone, speak about the service of the King, about false money, witches, hobgoblins, and whatnot—just to pour me two glasses of wine and send me to bed! It couldn't be more obvious. Weasel brought those instructions from the Corregidor, and at this very moment the Corregidor will be making his attempt on my wife! Who knows but that I may come upon him knocking at the mill door! Or inside the house! Who knows? But what am I saying? Do I doubt my fine girl? That is an offence to heaven! She could never—no! my Frasquita could never—! Impossible! Yet—what am I saying? Is there anything impossible under the sun? Didn't she marry me for all that she's so beautiful and I as ugly as sin?'

At this last thought tears started to the poor man's eyes. He halted the ass to calm himself. He dried his eyes, gave a deep sigh, took out his smoking set, bit and rolled a cigarette of black tobacco. Then he grasped his flint, tinder, and steel, and, after striking a few times, succeeded in lighting it.

At that moment he heard sounds of steps in the direction of the road nearly three hundred yards away. 'What a fool I am!' he muttered. 'Suppose the watch were out in search of me and I had happened to strike a light!' He covered the light and dismounted and hid behind the ass. But the ass evidently took another view of the situation and gave off a bray of satisfaction. 'Ah, drat you!' cried Tio Lucas, trying to close the beast's mouth with his bare hands. 'We're lost!' he told himself.' The proverb well says: "The worst curse of all is to deal with brute beasts"!' With this thought he remounted, urged the ass into motion, and galloped off in the opposite direction from that from which the answering bray had sounded.

Strangely enough, the unknown who was riding the other ass must have been just as alarmed as Tio Lucas himself. Or so one might think, since this person, whoever it was, also withdrew from the roadway, doubtless fearing that Tio Lucas was an Alguacil in the Corregidor's service, and scuttled off over the arable land on the other side.

The Miller rode on his way muttering and grumbling: 'What a night! What a world! What a turn my life has taken during the past hour! Alguacils out on pimps' errands! Alcaldes conspiring against my honour, asses braying at the wrong moment, and here, here inside me a miserable heart that has dared to doubt the noblest woman that ever God created!

75

Dear God! Grant that I soon reach home and find my Frasquita waiting!'

On and on went Tio Lucas across sown fields and copses—till at length, at something near eleven o'clock, he arrived without mishap at the mill.

'But what's this?' He ground his teeth. The door of the mill stood open!

CHAPTER XX

Doubt and Certainty

IT WAS open . . . and, on setting out that night, he had heard his wife shut, latch, and bolt it. And so no one but she could have opened it. But how? When? Why? Had she been taken in by some trick? Over-awed by an official order? Or had she indeed opened it of her own free will in connivance with the Corregidor?

He wondered what next would meet his eye. What awaited him inside the house? Had Frasquita run away? Had someone run off with her? Was she dead? Or in the arms of his enemy? 'The Corregidor felt sure I couldn't possibly be back till morning', he muttered gloomily. 'The village Alcalde's orders were to keep me there in irons if need be.' Was all this known to Frasquita? Was *she* in the plot? Or had she been the victim of a ruse, of violence, of an outrage?

All these torturing reflections passed through his mind in the short time it took to cross the little courtyard of the climbing vine.

The door of the house too was open. The first room —as is the way in country houses—was the kitchen. But the kitchen was empty. A huge fire was burning in the grate—the grate which he had left quenched

77

and cold, and which never used to be fired till well into December! And, to crown everything, from one of the hooks on the dresser hung a lighted lantern. . . . What did it all mean? And how could all these signs of company and life be reconciled with the deathly silence reigning through the house?

What had become of his wife?

At that very moment Tio Lucas's eye lighted on some garments hanging over the backs of two or three chairs placed around the fire. He stared fixedly at these, then he gave a groan so deep that it stuck in his throat and died into an inarticulate choking sob.

Poor man, he thought he was suffocating and raised his hands to his throat. Livid, convulsed, with staring eyes he regarded that array of clothing, struck with such horror as a condemned criminal feels on being confronted with the grave freshly dug for him. For what he saw there were the crimson cape, the three-cornered hat, the dove-grey coat and undercoat, the black silk breeches, the white stockings, the buckled shoes, the cane, rapier, and gloves of the accursed Corregidor. . . . What he gazed upon there meant for him the culmination of ignominy, the end of honour, the ruin of all his life's hopes.

The formidable blunderbuss still lay in the same corner where Frasquita had let it fall two hours before. Tio Lucas leapt upon it tigerishly and clutched it to his chest. He probed the barrel with the ramrod and saw that it was loaded. He looked at the gunflint and saw that it was in its proper place.

He turned then to the stairs leading to the room in which for so many years he had slept with Frasquita, and muttered in a low tone: 'That's where they are!' He advanced a step in that direction, but the next second paused to look all round and make sure no one was watching. 'Not a soul!' he whispered. 'Save God Himself . . . and He—it is His will!'

Strengthened thus in his purpose, he was about to take another step forward when his wandering eye lit upon a folded paper lying on the table. Seeing, lunging at it, and clutching it up with both hands were the work of a moment. The paper was the letter of appointment of Frasquita's nephew, signed by Don Eugenio de Zuniga y Ponce de Leon!

'This was the price for which she sold herself!' Lucas thought, thrusting the paper into his mouth to stifle his cries and feed his fury. 'I always feared she loved her own kindred better than me. Ah! We had no children—that's the cause of it all!' And the poor man was within an ace of bursting into tears once more.

Then his anger boiled up anew and he made a fiendish gesture which plainly said: 'Upstairs with you, man! Upstairs!'

He started climbing the stairs, one hand touching the stair-boards, the other gripping the blunderbuss, with that shameful paper held between his teeth. As if to bear out his natural suspicions, on coming in sight of the bedroom door—which was closed—he saw a few rays of light between the joints of the boards and through the keyhole.

'This is where they are!' he said again. And he

stopped for a second perhaps to digest this new draught of bitterness. Then he went on up the stairs, climbing till he reached the bedroom door. From inside the room not a sound could be heard. 'Suppose there's nobody there!' hope timidly suggested.

Just then—unlucky man!—he heard someone cough inside the room. The asthmatic cough of the Corregidor! There was no longer room for doubt! Not a straw remained for the lost man to clutch at!

Lucas grinned in the darkness—grinned horribly. It made his face gleam for a moment in the shadows like a lightning flash. What are all the flames that sinners feel in Hell to the fire that sears at times the heart of a living man?

Yet Lucas—of such rare substance was his nature —began to feel calm again as soon as he heard his enemy cough.

Reality wounds less keenly than doubt. As he himself had declared to Frasquita, immediately he lost that inmost faith which was the mainprop on which all his life rested, he began to change into a different man.

As with Shakespeare's Moor of Venice—with whom in describing his character we have already compared him—disillusionment was killing almost with one thrust all the love inside him, transfiguring at one swoop the very nature of his soul and causing him to view the world as a region new and un-familiar in which he had but newly arrived. The only difference was that Tio Lucas had a tempera-ment less tragic, less austere and more self-centred than Othello's.

A strange thing, but one peculiar to such situations! Doubt—or perhaps hope, which in this case is the same thing—still came back to torture him for a moment. . . .

'What if I am mistaken!' he thought. 'What if it were Frasquita coughing!'

Under the weight of his misfortune he was forgetting that he had seen the Corregidor's clothes beside the fire, that he had found the mill door open, that he had read the proof of his infamy. . . .

He stopped and looked through the keyhole, trembling with uncertainty and distress.

The angle of vision was only wide enough to include a narrow segment of the room—all around the bedhead. . . . Yet right in that small segment could be seen one end of the pillows and on the pillows the Corregidor's head!

Once more a devilish grin contracted the Miller's face. An onlooker might have thought he was happy again. 'I have got to the truth at last! Now let us think', he muttered, calmly straightening himself. And he went down the stairs again as cautiously as he had come up them.

'The matter is a delicate one—I must give it proper thought. I've time and enough for everything!' he whispered to himself as he descended. Reaching the kitchen, he sat down in the middle of the room and buried his forehead in his hands. He stayed thus a long time—then he was roused from his thought by feeling a light blow on one foot. It was the blunderbuss that had slid down from his knees. He took it for a sign.

'No! I say, No!' he said fiercely, taking aim with the weapon at some imaginary target. 'You won't do for me! Everyone would be sorry for them—and they'd hang *me*! A Corregidor is involved—no less! To kill a Corregidor is still a most heinous offence in Spain. They'd say I killed him from groundless jealousy and then stripped him and put him in my bed. . . . They'd say too that I killed my wife from mere suspicion! And they'd hang me! They'd surely hang me! Yet I should show myself of poor spirit and wit if at the close of my life I were to be pitied! They'd all laugh at me! They'd say my misfortunes were only to be expected—I being a hunchback and she so beautiful. No! What I must have is revenge, and after my revenge I must gloat, curl my lip, laugh;—yes, laugh out loud, laugh at everyone so that no one shall ever make fun of this hooped back of mine which I have contrived to make almost a thing of envy, but which would look grotesque enough on a gallows!'

In this vein Tio Lucas proceeded, perhaps not fully alive to where it was leading, and, now quite obsessed, picked up the pistol and began to pace about with arms clasped behind him and head lowered as if looking on the floor, on the earth, where lay the ruins of his life, for a way to avenge himself; as if intent on embodying his vengeance in some low and ludicrous jest at the expense of his wife and the Corregidor. This he did instead of seeking relief in justice, in a duel, or in forgiveness, in pious resignation, as, in his shoes, any other man would have done—any man, that is, of a temper less rebellious than his to any prompting of nature, humanity, and his own better feelings.

Suddenly his eyes stopped at the Corregidor's garments. Soon his pacing stopped too. Then by degrees there came over his face a look of pleasure, a merriment, an exultation which defied analysis. He began to laugh, to laugh immoderately in great gusts of laughter, but soundlessly so that they should not hear him upstairs. He shook all over like an epileptic and at the end was obliged to sink into a chair till the convulsion of bitter enjoyment passed.

As soon as he recovered he started to pull off his clothes with feverish haste. He put them all on the same chairs where the Corregidor's clothes were lying. Then he put on all that gentleman's garments from the buckled shoes to the three-cornered hat. He fastened on the rapier, flung the scarlet cape around his shoulders, and, taking up the cane and gloves, went out of the mill and turned in the direction of the city, swaying just like the Corregidor and repeating from time to time words which summarised all that was in his mind: 'The Corregidor's own lady—she too could tempt a man!'

CHAPTER XXI

On Guard, My Fine Gentleman!

WE LEAVE Tio Lucas for the present and pass to events at the mill between the time that Señora Frasquita was left alone there and the time when her husband came face to face with such an unfamiliar and shattering situation.

An hour had passed since Tio Lucas had gone off with Tonuelo. His anxious wife, who had made up her mind to sit up for her husband and was knitting in her bedroom upstairs, all at once heard pitiful cries close outside the house from the direction of the millstream.

'Help! Help! I'm drowning! Frasquita!' It was a man's voice raised with a dreadful note of desperation.

'Suppose it's Lucas!' Frasquita thought, filled, naturally, with terrible anxiety.

In the bedroom was a little door—the one Weasel had mentioned—which opened right over the middle of the millstream. Frasquita hastily threw this open, not recognising the appealing voice, and came face to face with the Corregidor just as he was scrambling out, dripping all over, from the racing waters.

'God forgive me! God forgive me!' stammered the old villain. 'I thought I was drowning!'

'How's this? You! What does this mean? How

dare you? What do you want here at this hour?'
cried Frasquita, more indignant than afraid, though
instinctively she backed away.

'Hush! Hush, woman!' hissed the Corregidor,
painfully hauling himself up into the room after her.
'I'll tell you the whole story. I've been within an ace
of drowning. The water swept me away like a feather!
Just look at the state I'm in!'

'You'll have to leave this house! You must go!'
Frasquita cried in a high voice. 'I don't want your
explanations. I understand everything only too well!
Suppose you *were* drowning? Did I ask you to come?
Ah! What a monstrous thing! It was for this then
that you had my husband called away!'

'Woman! Woman! Listen to me!'

'I won't listen! Be off this instant, my Lord
Corregidor! Off with you, or I won't answer for
your life!'

'What do you say?'

'It's exactly as you heard! My husband may not
be here but I know how to take care of myself! Off
with you where you came from—if you don't want
me to push you back in the water with my own
hands!'

'My dear! My dear! Don't shout like that—I'm not
deaf!' said the old rake. 'I've a good reason for
coming at this time. I come to release Tio Lucas
who was arrested by mistake by some country
Alcalde. But, first of all, I must ask you to dry these
clothes of mine. I'm drenched to the bone!'

'Be off, I tell you!'

'Hush, you silly woman! Don't you realise—?

Look, here I bring your nephew's appointment.
Light the light and we'll talk. Now! While my clothes
are drying I'll bed down in this room.'

'Indeed! You say you came here for my sake? You
say that such-and-such was why you had my Lucas
arrested? And you bring your letter of appointment
and everything? Merciful heaven! What on earth
does this old fright take me for?'

'Frasquita! I am the Corregidor!'

'I wouldn't care if you were the King! It means
nothing to me! I am my husband's wife and mistress
of my house! Do you think I'm afraid of any Corregidor? I can go to Madrid or the ends of the earth to
get redress against the insolent old man who drags
his high office in the dirt like this! Or—what is more
to the point—tomorrow I can throw on my mantilla
and go and see her Ladyship your wife!'

'You'll do nothing of the sort!' cried the Corregidor, losing patience, or changing his tactics.
'You'll do nothing of the sort! I'll shoot you if you
persist in shutting your ears to reason. . . .'

'Shoot me!' repeated Frasquita in a curiously low
voice.

'Yes, shoot you. . . . And, even if you did what you
propose it wouldn't do me the least harm. I happen
to have dropped the hint in the city that I would be
out tonight after malefactors. . . . Don't be foolish
then. Be nice to me! . . . I adore you!'

'My Lord Corregidor, did you say "shoot me"?'
Frasquita asked again and again, holding her arms
behind her and thrusting her body forward as if
about to fling herself on the enemy.

'Yes, if you don't give over I'll shoot you, and so make an end of your threats—and your accursed beauty too. . . .' A sudden tremor of fear shook the Corregidor and he pulled out a pair of pocket pistols.

'So then! Pistols too! And in the other pocket my nephew's appointment!' Frasquita looked him up and down. 'Then, sir, the choice is made. Wait a moment—I'll light a light.' She made rapidly for the stairs and descended them in three bounds.

The Corregidor took up the light and followed her anxious that she should not escape; but he was obliged to take the stairs more slowly. So he reached the kitchen below just in time to run full tilt into Frasquita on her way back.

'So! You said you were going to shoot me, eh?' said the dauntless woman, taking a step back. 'Well then, on guard, my fine gentleman! I'm ready for you!' And she thrust under his nose the formidable blunderbuss that has already figured in the story.

'Stop, wretched woman! What are you going to do?' the Corregidor cried, terror-stricken.' My talk of shooting was only a joke! Look—the pistols are not loaded. On the other hand, what I said about the appointment was true. . . . Here you are . . . Take it! A little present from me. . . . It's yours. No return is looked for—none, absolutely none!' Trembling he laid the document down on the table.

'Good!' said Frasquita. 'Tomorrow it will do to light the fire for cooking my husband's breakfast. I don't want anything from you at all. If my nephew ever *does* leave Estella it will be to come and stamp on the wicked hand that wrote his name on that disgraceful paper! There! I've had my say. Now get out of my house! Take yourself off! Away with you! At once! . . . I feel my temper rising!'

The Corregidor did not answer. He had turned a livid, bluish colour. His eyes turned up, and a fit of feverish trembling shook him all over. Then his teeth began chattering and he fell to the ground, seized with a frightful convulsion. The shock of the millstream, the drenched clothes, the violent scene in the bedroom, his terror of the blunderbuss which Frasquita was pointing at him, had drained away his last strength.

'I'm dying!' he muttered hoarsely. 'Call Weasel! . . . Call Weasel! He's close by—in the ravine. I mustn't die . . . not in this house!' He stopped, exhausted, his eyes closed, and he lay like one dead.

'And he will die, too!' Frasquita suddenly realised. 'Lord! This is as bad as can be! What shall I do with this man in my house? What would people say if he died here? What would Lucas say? What excuse could I make as I opened the door to him myself? No! I can't stay here with him. I must find my husband! What if I give people something to talk about? That's better than losing my good name!'

Her mind made up, she dropped the blunderbuss, went out into the yard, took out the remaining ass, saddled it somehow or other, opened the great gate of the yard, mounted in one leap for all her largeness of body, and rode off by the ravine.

'Weasel! Weasel!' she called as she came near it.

'Here I am!' At last the Alguacil answered,

showing himself from behind a hedge. 'Is that Señora Frasquita?'

'Yes, it is. Go to the mill and look after your master—he's dying!'

'What's that you say? A likely tale!'

'I'm speaking the truth, Weasel!'

'And you, by the saints! Where are you off to at this hour?'

'I? . . . Hands off, rascal! I'm off to the city for a doctor.' With this Frasquita urged on the ass with a dig of her heel and aimed a passing kick at Weasel. She did not take the road to the city, as she had said, but made towards the neighbouring village.

Weasel took no stock of this circumstance. He strode back with long strides to the mill, and as he went muttered to himself: 'Go for a doctor, eh? The wretched woman might well do that! . . . What an unlucky man he is, though! A fine time to fall ill! Heaven gives him a titbit and he can't get his teeth into it!'

CHAPTER XXII

Weasel Plays Many Parts

WHEN Weasel reached the mill the Corregidor was beginning to come round and had managed to lift himself up from the ground. On the floor beside him stood the the lighted candle which he had brought down from the bedroom.

'Has she gone?' was the Corregidor's first sentence.

'Who?'

'That she-devil! I mean . . . the Miller's wife. . . .'

'Yes, my Lord, she's gone, and I don't think she's in a very good humour.'

'Oh dear, Weasel! I'm dying . . .!'

'Eh? What's that your Lordship's saying? By all that's living!'

'I fell into the millstream and caught a chill. My bones and flesh are parting with the cold!'

'Well, indeed! So that's all we get out of this!'

'Weasel! Mind your tongue!'

'I'm not saying a word, sir.'

'That's as well. Get me out of this fix.'

'I will—right away! Your Lordship shall see— I'll put things right in no time!'

So saying, he snatched up the light with one hand and thrust the other under the Corregidor's arm, helping him up to the bedroom. There he stripped off all his master's clothes, put him to bed, ran out of the mill to the pit where the grapes were pressed, gathered an armful of faggots, returned to the kitchen, made a huge fire, brought all his master's clothes downstairs, arranged them on the backs of two or three chairs, lit the oil lamp, hung it up on the kitchen rack, and finally climbed back upstairs to the bedroom.

'How do we feel now?' he asked the Corregidor, holding the candle high so as to see his master's face the better.

'Oh, wonderful!' The Corregidor scowled. 'I feel a perspiration coming on. Tomorrow I'll have you hanged, Weasel!'

'What for, my Lord?'

'You dare ask? If only I'd known that by following out your precious plan I'd end up all by myself in this bed—yes, and get a second holy baptism into the bargain! I'm hanging you in the morning for sure!'

'Will your Lordship tell me one thing? Did Señora Frasquita—?'

'Señora Frasquita would have murdered me. That's all I've gained by your advice! I tell you, you're hanging in the morning—first thing!'

'Hardly, my Lord Corregidor', said the Alguacil.

'Why do you say that, you insolent rogue? Because you see me laid on my back?'

'No, my Lord. I mean that Señora Frasquita can't be as bad as your Lordship says. She's gone to the city to fetch a doctor.'

'God in heaven! Are you sure she's gone to the

city?' cried the Corregidor, more dismayed than ever.

'Well, that's what she told me.'

'Then run, Weasel, run! Ah! I'm ruined beyond cure! Do you know why Señora Frasquita's gone to the city? To tell everything to my wife! To tell her I'm here! Heavens! Heavens! How was I to foresee this? I thought she had gone to the village to fetch her husband and, as I had him there under good guard, what did I care about her going there? But to go to the city! Run, Weasel, run! You're fast on your feet. Run and prevent my utter ruin! Stop that dreadful woman entering my house!'

'And you won't hang me if I do?' the Alguacil asked with a touch of irony.

'Of course not! I'll make you a present of some good wearable shoes that don't fit me. You shall have anything you wish.'

'Then I'm off like a bird! Have a good sleep, my Lord. Inside half-an-hour I'll be back here, leaving that woman behind me in jail. Not for nothing am I swifter on the road than any pack-animal!' And Weasel hurried downstairs.

It was, of course, while the Alguacil was away on this errand that Lucas was in the mill and saw certain sights through the keyhole.

We now leave the Corregidor sweating in a strange bed and Weasel running towards the city (where Tio Lucas was to follow him so soon after in three-cornered hat and crimson cape) and just as speedily make for the village after the valiant Frasquita.

CHAPTER XXIII

Again the Open Country and Those Voices!

THE one notable occurrence during Frasquita's trip from the mill to the village was her sudden alarm at sighting a shadowy figure striking a tinder-box in the middle of a ploughed field.

'What if it's one of the Corregidor's bailiffs? What if he stops me?' thought Frasquita.

At that moment a sound of braying was heard from the same direction. 'Asses out at this hour!' she muttered. 'And yet there's no farmstead or small-holding hereabouts! Good life! but the goblins are out and about tonight and no mistake! It couldn't be, I suppose, my little Lucas's ass? No! Whatever would Lucas be doing in the middle of the night, dismounted, and right off the road? No doubt it's someone on the look-out!' Her own ass chose that moment to bray an answer to the first ass. 'Quiet, you devil!' Frasquita hissed, and jabbed the pin of her ochavo coin brooch right in the animal's withers. Then, for fear of some unwelcome encounter, she rode the beast off the highway and began trotting it across the ploughed fields. Without further incident she reached the outskirts of the village. It was then about eleven o'clock.

CHAPTER XXIV

A King of the Old School

WHEN Tonuelo, after a discreet knock, entered the mayoral bedroom he found his Worship deep in a drunken sleep back-to-back with his wife, the two thus forming, as the immortal Quevedo observes somewhere, the figure of the two-headed eagle of Austria. At once he informed his master that Señora Frasquita—'her from the mill'—wished to speak to him.

We need not record all the grunts and oaths that accompanied our homespun Alcalde's waking up and struggling into his clothes. We pass to the moment when Frasquita saw him come in stretching himself and flexing his muscles like a gymnast and heard him say through a protracted yawn: 'A good day to you, Señora Frasquita! What brings you to this part of the world? Didn't Tonuelo tell you to stay at the mill? Is this your idea of obeying the law?'

'I've got to see my Lucas!' insisted Frasquita. 'I must see him at once! Let him know that his wife is here!'

' "Got to!" "Got to!" You forget that you are talking to the King!'

'Don't speak to me of Kings, Master Juan, I haven't come here to listen to nonsense! You know very well what I've been through! You know very well why you locked up my husband!'

'I know nothing of the sort, Señora Frasquita. And your husband—he's not locked up but peacefully asleep in this house where he's been treated as I always treat respectable people. Tonuelo! Tonuelo! Go to the barn and tell Tio Lucas to get up and come here quickly! Come now, Señora, tell me what the matter is! Were you afraid of spending the night alone?'

'Don't be so brazen, Master Juan. I'm not partial to your little speeches either in joke or otherwise, as you well know. As to what the matter is, that's plain enough surely! You and my Lord Corregidor wanted to ruin me, but you have failed utterly! Here am I with no reason at all to blush or hang my head, while the Corregidor is back there in the mill at death's door!'

'At death's door? The Corregidor?' The Alcalde's voice almost broke. 'Lady! Do you realise what you are saying?'

'I fully realise! He fell into the millstream and nearly drowned, and now he's caught a chill on the lungs or something. That's for her Ladyship his wife to worry about! I come to fetch my husband. Then the pair of us can set off tomorrow for Madrid! There I shall tell the King . . .!'

'The Devil! Damnation!' muttered Master Juan Lopez. 'Manuela! Come here, wench! Go and saddle the little mule. Señora Frasquita, I'm off to the mill! Heaven help you if you've done any harm to my Lord Corregidor!'

'Master Alcalde! Master Alcalde!' Tonuelo ran in with a face white as death. 'Tio Lucas isn't in the

95

barn! I can't see his ass in the manger either! And somebody's left the yard gate open! It looks as if the bird has flown!'

'What d'you say?' shouted Master Juan Lopez.

'Blessed Virgin! What will happen at the mill? Let's be on our way, Master Alcalde! Lose no time! My husband will kill the Corregidor if he finds him there!'

'You think Tio Lucas is at the mill?'

'Where else? What's more, on my way here I passed him without knowing. It was he, no doubt, that struck the tinder-box in the middle of the ploughed field. Great heavens! To think that brute beasts should have more sense than human beings! Would you believe it, Master Juan?—our two asses recognised and signalled to each other whereas Lucas and I did neither. Instead we thought each other scouts for the Corregidor and ran!'

'Your Lucas is in a pretty mess!' said the Alcalde. 'Come, let's be on our way, and then we'll see how we shall deal with the pair of you! I'm not the sort to be trifled with! I am the King! Not, I mean, a king like the one we have now in Madrid—that's to say, in the Prado—but like that one in Seville once called Pedro the Cruel. Manuela! Here, Manuela, fetch me my stick and tell your mistress I am going out.'

The maid did as she was told. She was, by the way, too good a girl for the Alcalde's lady and, in perhaps another sense, for the Alcalde too. Master Lopez's ass by now being saddled, Frasquita and he set out for the mill, followed by the trusty Tonuelo.

CHAPTER XXV

The Weasel's Star

MEANWHILE Weasel had returned to the mill after having searched for Frasquita in all the streets of the city.

The astute Alguacil had paid a passing call at the Town Hall where he found everything quiet. The great doors stood open as at noonday, as they always did when authority had gone out in the discharge of its sacred duties. On the stairway landing and in the ante-room some other Alguacils awaiting their master's return were uneasily dozing. At the sound of Weasel's entrance they roused themselves and asked him, as the master's deputy: 'Is his Lordship here?'

'Of course not! Be quiet, all of you! I'm here to learn if anything has happened.'

'Nothing whatever.'

'What about her Ladyship?'

'She's shut herself up in her apartments.'

'Didn't a woman come in just now?'

'Nobody has been here all night. . . .'

'Well, let nobody in, whoever he be and whatever he say! Not for any reason! No matter who comes asking for my Lord or my Lady—seize him and put him in jail!'

'They must be after some very big birds tonight!' one of the bailiffs remarked as though to nobody in particular.

'Quite a hunt!' put in another.

'With a capital H!' Weasel replied gravely. 'You can guess how important it is since my Lord Corregidor and I act as beaters ourselves! So long, then! and good hunting! Keep your eyes peeled.'

'God go with you, Master Bastian!' they all cried, bobbing and bowing to the Weasel.

'My star is in eclipse!' he muttered to himself when he was outside the Town Hall again. 'Even women fool me now! The Miller's wife was on her way to the village to fetch her husband—not off to the city! Poor Weasel! What's become of your powers of scent?'

He was right to mourn his declining powers of scent, for he quite failed to get wind of a man who that very moment darted into hiding behind a clump of willows near the ravine, muttering to himself inside his greatcoat—or rather scarlet cape: 'Look out, man! Here's Weasel! He mustn't see you at any price!'

It was Tio Lucas on his way to the city. He had on the Corregidor's clothes and every now and then kept saying to himself with malicious gusto: 'Yes, indeed! The Corregidor's lady too could tempt a man!'

Weasel went by without seeing him and the sham Corregidor came out of his hiding-place and went on his way. Some time later he entered the city. A few minutes afterwards the Alguacil arrived at the mill, as the reader already knows.

CHAPTER XXVI

Reaction

THE Corregidor still lay in bed in the attitude in which Tio Lucas had seen him through the keyhole.

'How I've sweated, Weasel!' he said as soon as the Alguacil was back in the room. 'What of Señora Frasquita? Did you find her? Is she with you? Did she speak to her Ladyship?'

'The Miller's wife tricked me', Weasel answered in a sad voice. 'Tricked me like a simpleton. She didn't go to the city but to the village—looking for her husband. Forgive my stupidity, my Lord . . .'

'But that's better! Better than anything!' said the Corregidor, and his eyes glinted wickedly. 'That puts everything right! Before the daylight comes again Tio Lucas and Señora Frasquita will be on their way to the Inquisition's prison, bound back to back, and there they'll rot with never a soul to tell tonight's adventure to! Bring me my clothes, Weasel. They must be dry by now. Bring them and help me dress! The lover is about to turn into the Corregidor . . .!'

Weasel went down to the kitchen to fetch the clothes.

CHAPTER XXVII

In the King's Name!

MEANWHILE Señora Frasquita, Master Juan Lopez, and Tonuelo were nearing the mill, which they reached a few minutes later.

'I'll go in first!' our rustic Alcalde announced. 'I'll show them who represents law and order here! Follow me, Tonuelo! You, Señora Frasquita, stay here at the door till I call you.' Then he marched in under the grapevine to where a band of moonlight showed up a man—a hunchback, it seemed—in the familiar garb of the Miller—grey cloth waistcoat and breeches, black sash, blue stockings, Murcian velour cap, with a countryman's capote thrown over one shoulder.

'It's he!' shouted the Alcalde. 'Give yourself up, Tio Lucas!'

Velour Cap made to dart back into the mill.

'Ah, would you!' It was Tonuelo now. He leaped upon the man, seized him round the neck and, driving a knee into the small of his back, sent him rolling on the ground. At that moment a wild being of quite another sort leaped upon Tonuelo and, hauling him by his belt, dragged him down on the stone flags and began slapping and pummelling him vigorously. This was Frasquita. She kept shouting: 'Ruffian! Let go my Lucas!'

Just then another figure appeared, leading in an ass from somewhere on the right. He shoved resolutely between the two strugglers, intent on rescuing Tonuelo. It was Weasel. He had taken the village Alguacil for his master in the darkness. 'Lady! Treat my master with respect!' he said, and with a shove from his shoulders he pushed her down on top of Tonuelo. Madam, finding herself, as it were, between two fires, at once let drive at Weasel a tremendous thrust in the pit of the stomach and fairly bowled him over, for all his lanky height. And with him a whole quartet of bodies was now rolling on the ground.

Meanwhile Master Juan Lopez was exerting himself to prevent the supposed Tio Lucas from getting to his feet. He had one foot firmly planted in the other's ribs.

'Weasel! Help! Help! In the King's name! I am the Corregidor!' yelled Don Eugenio at last, feeling the Alcalde's hoof shod in a bullhide sandal pressing on him heavily.

'The Corregidor! Bless me! So it is!' gasped Master Juan Lopez in utter amazement.

'The Corregidor!' they all echoed. At the same time four sprawling figures scrambled to their feet.

'I'll put you all in irons!' screamed Don Eugenio. 'I'll send you all to the gallows!'

'B-but, my Lord . . . ', began Master Juan Lopez, falling on his knees. 'P-pardon me, your Excellency, for ill-treating you. How was I to recognise your Lordship in such common dress?'

'Oaf!' retorted the Corregidor. 'I had to put on

something! Don't you know they robbed me of my own clothes? Don't you know that a band of thieves sent here by Tio Lucas—'

'That's a lie!' cried Frasquita.

'You listen to me, Señora Frasquita', said the Alguacil, beckoning her aside. 'By the leave of the Lord Corregidor and all present . . .! If you don't come to some arrangement we'll be hanged every one beginning with Tio Lucas!'

'Why, what's the matter?' asked Frasquita.

'Tio Lucas is traipsing through the city right now dressed up as the Corregidor . . . and—Heaven only knows!—in that disguise he may be in her Ladyship's room at this very moment.' And the Alguacil told her in brief what the reader knows already.

'Jesu!' exclaimed Frasquita. 'Then my husband believes me dishonoured! He's gone to the city to avenge me! Let's be off at once! Away to the city and clear my name in my husband's eyes!'

'Off to the city! And stop that man speaking to my wife—telling her all the nonsense that occurs to his fertile fancy!' The Corregidor pressed up to one of the asses. 'Take my foot and help me mount, Master Alcalde.'

'To the city! Yes!'

'To the city—by all means!' Weasel said, 'and Heaven grant, my Lord Corregidor, that Tio Lucas has been satisfied with just speaking to her Ladyship!'

'What's that you say, you rogue?' thundered Don Eugenio. 'Do you think that boor capable . . .?'

'Of anything!' answered Frasquita.

CHAPTER XXVIII

Ave Maria Purissima! Half-past Twelve and All Clear!

THE night-watchmen were raising this cry through the streets of the city when the Miller's wife and the Corregidor, each on one of the Miller's asses, with Master Juan Lopez on his mule and the two Alguacils on foot, arrived at the main door of the Town Hall.

The door was closed.

For both governors and governed, it seemed to declare, business was over for the day.

'This is bad!' muttered Weasel to himself. And he banged the great knocker two or three times.

A long time passed; no one opened or in any way answered the summons. Mistress Frasquita had turned paler than wax. The Corregidor gnawed the fingernails of each hand nervously.

Nobody spoke a word.

Bang! Bang! Bang! Blow upon blow thundered on the door of the Town Hall, applied alternately by the two Alguacils and Master Juan Lopez. They might have spared themselves—there was no response. No one came to the door. Not a creature stirred.

All that could be heard was the light sound of the spouting of a fountain that stood in the patio of the building. And in this way passed entire minutes, long as eternities. At last—it was about one o'clock— a little window on the third floor opened, and a woman's voice said, 'Who is it?'

'It's the nurse', whispered Weasel.

'It is I!' answered Don Eugenio. 'Open the door!'

There was a moment of silence.

'Who did you say it was?' at last the nurse said.

'Why don't you listen? I am your master! . . . the Corregidor! . . .'

There was another pause.

'God be with you!' came again the good woman's voice. 'But my master came home an hour ago and went to bed directly. You folk had better do the same and sleep off the wine inside you!' And the window closed with a thud.

Frasquita covered her face with her hands.

'Wench!' thundered the Corregidor, beside himself. 'Don't you hear me telling you to open the door? Do you not hear that it's I? Do you want me to hang you as well?'

The window went up again. 'Now what's all this? Who is shouting like that?'

'I am the Corregidor!'

'Tell me another! Haven't I said that my Lord Corregidor came in before twelve? And that with my own eyes I saw him let himself in to her Ladyship's suite? Are you trying to make a fool of me? Just you wait and see what happens to you!'

As she spoke the door suddenly opened and a swarm of servants and retainers, each armed with a cudgel, rushed upon those outside, shouting furiously, 'Here we are now. Where is the fellow who says he is the Corregidor? Where is the clown?—the drunkard?'

And with this began the devil's own melée in the pitch darkness, in which the Corregidor, Weasel, Master Juan Lopez, and Tonuelo each took two or three blows apiece. It was the second rough-handling which that night's adventure had cost Don Eugenio —not counting the drenching he was given in the millstream.

Frasquita, separated some distance from the whirling tangle of men, was in tears for the first time in her life. . . .

'Lucas! Lucas!' she was sobbing. 'How could you doubt me? How could you put your arms round another woman? Ah! Nothing can end our unhappiness!'

CHAPTER XXIX

The Moon Shines Through the Clouds

'WHAT'S all this uproar about?' A voice said at last, a voice calm, majestic and melodious, that sounded high above the fracas. They all looked up and saw a woman in a black dress looking down from the second-storey window. 'Her Ladyship!' the Town Hall servants hissed, and the thudding sound of falling cudgels instantly ceased.

'My wife!' stammered the Corregidor.

'Let in those country folk', said her Ladyship, and added as an afterthought, 'My Lord Corregidor gives them leave.'

The servants stood aside, and the Corregidor and his party passed through the doorway and made their way upstairs. Never did condemned criminal mount the scaffold with such faltering steps and hangdog looks as the Corregidor climbed the stairway in his own house. And yet so proud and egoistic was he by nature that the thought of his dishonour was already beginning to loom larger than all the misfortunes that had come upon him and all the other ridiculous features of the situation in which he found himself.

'Before everything', he said to himself as he trod

the stairs, 'before everything I am a Zuniga and a Ponce de Leon! Let them look to themselves if they've forgotten that! Let my Lady beware if she has besmirched my name!'

CHAPTER XXX

A Lady of Quality

HER LADYSHIP received her husband and his retinue of countryfolk in the principal reception room of the Town Hall. She stood alone, her eyes fastened on the doorway.

She was, without doubt, a supremely noble lady, still quite young, and beautiful in a quiet, rather austere fashion, a fitter model for a Christian than a pagan painter, and her dress had all the sober dignity favoured by the taste of the time. The gown she wore, the narrow, rather short skirt and the high, full sleeves were of fine black alpaca wool. A creamy white lace shawl draped her superb shoulders, and the longest of black tulle gloves covered arms like alabaster. She stood fanning herself regally with an enormous fan, which had come from the Philippine Islands, and held in her other hand a lace handkerchief, and the precise way its four corners fitted over each other somehow gave a crowning touch to the lady's immaculateness.

This handsome woman had about her something of a queen, but something more of an abbess, and inspired reverence and awe in all who saw her. For the rest, the grandness of her costume—considering the lateness of the hour—her proud and serious bearing, and the multitude of lights in the salon proved that her Ladyship had done everything to give the scene a touch of drama and pomp and thus show up all the gross vulgarity in her husband's escapade.

This lady, be it known, moreover, was by name and title the Lady Mercedes Carrillo de Albornoz y Espinosa de los Monteros, and was daughter, niece, greatniece, great grandniece, as well as niece twenty times removed, to that famous city, being a direct descendant of its illustrious Conquistadors. For purely material reasons her family had induced her to marry the rich and ageing Corregidor, and her Ladyship, who would otherwise have been a nun —her natural bent having always been for the cloister —had consented to the painful sacrifice. At this time she had two children by her rakish husband, and it was a common rumour in the town that a third was on the way.

CHAPTER XXXI

An Eye for an Eye

'MERCEDES!' cried the Corregidor, confronting his wife. 'I demand to know at once—!'

'Hello, Tio Lucas! Are you here?' said her Ladyship, interrupting him. 'Is everything all right at the mill?'

'Madam! I'm not here to jest!' The Corregidor's voice was thick with anger. 'Before I start any explaining on my side I insist on knowing whether my honour has been—'

'That's nothing to do with me! Did you by chance leave it in my charge?'

'Yes, my lady, I did!' replied Don Eugenio. 'Wives are always the repositories of their husbands' honours.'

'Very well then, Tio Lucas, ask your wife. She is listening to us at this very moment.'

Frasquita, who had all this time been standing on the threshold, gave a sort of cry.

'Come in, Madam, and sit down', said her Ladyship, turning in her queenliest manner to address Frasquita. At the same time she walked to the sofa. The large-hearted Frasquita divined at once all the noble forbearance under the calm of that wronged—

perhaps doubly wronged—wife. And so, rising to a similar level herself, she mastered her natural impulse and kept gravely silent. Naturally enough, in the sure knowledge of her own innocence and strength, she was in no hurry to justify herself. She was eager indeed to lay charges—grave charges—but certainly not against her Ladyship. The one she wished to settle scores with was Tio Lucas—but *he* was not there.

'Señora Frasquita', the noble lady repeated, seeing that the Miller's wife stayed where she was, 'I have asked you to come in and sit down.' This second invitation was spoken in a friendlier, more sympathetic tone than the first. No doubt her Ladyship's instinct told her, on the first full glance at Frasquita, that here was no common peasant woman, here was someone perhaps as sorely tried as herself, and that, like her own, this woman's trials sprang from the Corregidor.

So the two women exchanged the most friendly and forgiving glances, even though they regarded each other as rivals twice over. Almost in spite of themselves, each felt her heart go out to the other as to a sister found again after a long separation. In just such a manner might the pure white snowy peaks of two distant Alps flash a salute to each other in the sunlight.

Conscious of this new feeling, Frasquita drew herself up, stepped proudly into the salon, and seated herself on the edge of a chair. During her passage through the mill, knowing that she would have to appear before people of quality, she had touched herself up a little, and put on a black flannel mantilla with velvet bobbles that became her greatly. She had quite an air about her, had Frasquita.

All through this scene the Corregidor stayed quite silent. Frasquita's cry and entry upon the stage had fairly taken the wind out of his sails. That woman instilled more terror in him than his own wife!

'Come now, my dear Tio Lucas', her Ladyship went on, turning towards her Lord. 'Here is Señora Frasquita for you. Now's the time to ask your question! Now's the time to ask about your honour!'

'For the love of Heaven, Mercedes!' almost shrieked the Corregidor. 'Take care! You do not know to what lengths I can go! Once again I beseech you—stop this nonsense and tell me what has happened while I've been away. Where is that man?'

'Who? My husband? My husband is just getting out of bed—and should be here very soon.'

'Getting out of bed?' Don Eugenio's voice rose again.

'Does that surprise you? Where now would you have a respectable man at this hour but in his bed and sleeping with his lawful wife, as God wills?'

'Mercedes, my love! Take care what you say! Remember, people are listening! Remember, I am the Corregidor!'

Her Ladyship rose to her feet. 'Don't raise your voice at me, Tio Lucas! or I'll have the Alguacils throw you in the cells!'

'Throw me in the cells! Me! The Corregidor of this city!'

'The Corregidor of this city, the representative of the Law, the deputy of the King', her Ladyship declaimed in a voice high enough to override her Lord's sibilant one, 'came home at the due time to repose from the high duties of his office, and then in the morning resume the protection of citizens' honour and lives, the preserving of the sanctity of their property and the modesty of their womenfolk. And this by making sure that no man, whether disguised as the Corregidor or otherwise, entered the room of another's wife—that no man took womanly virtue at a disadvantage in unwary slumber, that no man abused her chaste sleep. . . .'

'Mercedes, my love! Whatever are you talking about?' the Corregidor hissed through nearly clenched teeth. 'If such things have really come to pass in my house I say you are a slut, a faithless wretch, a wanton!'

'To whom is he talking—this fellow?' In a voice full of disdain her Ladyship enquired of the by-standers. 'Who is this madman—this drunken sot? I can't think it's a respectable miller like Tio Lucas, even though he is wearing his country habit. Master Juan Lopez, believe me', she went on, appealing to the village Alcalde who could hardly look at her for awe, 'my husband, the Corregidor of the city, came home two hours ago with his three-cornered hat, his scarlet cape, his cavalier's rapier, and his staff of authority. The servants and Alguacils you see around us all rose to their feet and bowed to him as they watched him pass through the door, up the stairs, and through the vestibule. At once all the doors were closed, and from that time not a soul has come in until you people arrived. Is that the truth?'

She appealed to the servants. 'Tell him, will you?'

'It's Gospel truth! It surely is!' the nurse, the servants, and the Alguacils replied in chorus, for all of them, in a group near the salon door, were spectators at the scene.

'Be off, the whole pack of you!' screamed the Corregidor, foaming with rage. 'Weasel! Weasel! Come and arrest these rascals that show no respect for me! Put them under lock and key! String them up, I say!' No Weasel, however, came forward.

The Lady Mercedes continued. 'What is more, sir'—she had changed her tone now, condescended to look at her husband and to treat him as such, feeling perhaps a misgiving that the jest could be carried to irreparable extremes—'say that you *are* my husband. . . . Suppose you *are* Don Eugenio de Zuniga y Ponce de Leon . . .'

'I *am*!'

'Suppose, what is more, that some blame *does* attach to me for having taken for you the man who came into my room dressed as the Corregidor—'

'Shameless creature!' croaked the old man, thrusting a hand to his sword-hilt but encountering only the Miller's sash in its place.

Frasquita hid her face in one side of her mantilla to hide the burning anger and jealousy that showed there.

'Suppose anything you like', went on the Lady Mercedes with a baffling imperturbability. 'Tell me, my fine sir, would you have the right to complain? Could you play the prosecutor and accuse me? Could you be judge and condemn me? Do you come here from church, by any chance? Do you come straight from the confessional? or from hearing Mass? Where *do* you come from, dressed as you are? And in the company of that lady? Where have you spent half the night?'

'By your leave', broke in Frasquita, almost bounding to her feet and putting herself boldly between her Ladyship and her husband. The latter, who was about to say something, stopped open-mouthed on seeing that Frasquita was about to open fire. Nevertheless, it was the Lady Mercedes who spoke first. 'Madame, please do not tire yourself with giving me explanations. I don't ask you to— far from it! But here comes one who has the right to ask. Make things right with him!'

At the same time the door of a side room opened and in the doorway appeared Tio Lucas, still dressed from head to foot in the Corregidor's clothes, with cane, gloves, and rapier, just as though he were making a formal appearance in the Council Chamber.

CHAPTER XXXII

Faith Moves Mountains

'A VERY good evening to you all!' the newcomer announced, sweeping off his three-cornered hat and speaking with lips indrawn just like Don Eugenio. Then he immediately advanced into the middle of the room swaying from side to side, and went and kissed her Ladyship's hand.

The bystanders were stupefied. Tio Lucas's resemblance to the real Corregidor was miraculous. The crowd of servants, and even Master Juan Lopez himself, couldn't help laughing aloud. This new affront nettled Don Eugenio and he flung himself venomously towards Tio Lucas. But Frasquita, intervening, sent the Corregidor reeling back with, so to speak, no more than a push from her little finger. To avoid falling with him and thereby adding to the ludicrousness of the spectacle, her Ladyship stepped back and let him fall to the ground without a word. The fair Miller's wife was clearly more than a match for the Corregidor.

Tio Lucas turned deathly pale on seeing his wife so near, but quickly mastered himself. He gave a smile—more like a grimace of pain—and, clutching at his heart as if to stop if from breaking, said in his mock Corregidor voice: 'God keep you, Frasquita!

Have you sent the letter of appointment to your nephew?'

The effect upon Frasquita was electrifying. She flung back her mantilla, raised her head with the proud gesture of a lioness and fixed eyes like daggers on Lucas. 'I despise you, Lucas!' She seemed to spit the words at him. Onlookers thought that she had in very truth spat at him, so vehement was her gesture, her bearing, the tone of her voice.

The Miller's face changed completely at this outburst from his wife. An exultation, akin to that which accompanies religious faith, surged up in his soul and submerged him in a flood of enlightenment and joy. He forgot in an instant all he had seen, real or imaginary, at the mill, and cried out, tears in his eyes, with intensest feeling: 'So you really are my Frasquita! My Frasquita!'

'No!' cried Frasquita passionately. 'I am not your Frasquita! Think of your deeds of tonight and remind yourself of what you have done to a heart that loved you so!' And she broke into tears. It was like the sudden crumbling and thaw of a glacier. Her Ladyship, unable to suppress her feelings, went to her and put her arms very tenderly around her shoulders. Frasquita embraced her in turn without knowing what she did, and between her sobs murmured like a child seeking comforting mother's arms: 'O my lady! My lady! I am so unhappy!'

'Ah, you imagine things are much worse than they are', her Ladyship replied, weeping pretty freely herself by this time.

'Meanwhile it's I who am the unhappy one', Tio

Lucas began moaning quietly, fighting hard against tears.

'What about me!' wailed Don Eugenio, finally unmanned by the contagious weeping all round him, or possibly seeing in tears a way out of his predicament. 'I am a villain! A monster! An utter libertine who has only got what he deserves!' And he began a doleful bleating, hiding his face in the portly midriff of Master Juan Lopez. Certain onlookers began loudly competing with him, and the whole episode looked like ending without a single one of the several suspects having to say a word to clear his name.

CHAPTER XXXIII

How About Yourself?

TIO LUCAS was the first to surface from that flood of tears. That glimpse he had caught through the bedroom keyhole at the mill suddenly recurred to him. 'Now, sirs, to business!' he suddenly exclaimed.

'Never mind business, as you call it, Tio Lucas', said her Ladyship. 'Your wife here is innocent.'

'Yes, I know—but—'

'No buts, if you please! Just let her say a word, and you'll see how you've wronged her. One look at her and my heart cried out she was a saint! No matter what you have told me!'

'Very well then—let her speak.'

'I won't speak!' Frasquita cried. 'You are the one who should speak! The truth is that it was you—' She stopped short, abashed by a returning awe of her Ladyship.

But Lucas was quick to retort: 'What about *you*?' He was deep-sunk in doubt once more.

The Corregidor too was reminded of his wrongs. 'The affair does not concern that woman!' he snapped at Tio Lucas. 'It concerns you and that lady there.' He gestured impatiently at his own wife. 'Ah, Mercedes my dear! Who would have thought that you—'

119

'I? And what of you?' retorted her Ladyship, piercing him with a look. And for the next few moments the angry pair tossed backwards and forwards the same recriminatory phrases. 'You mean *you* did!' 'Indeed I mean *you* did!' 'Pardon me but—!' 'How *can* you say—!' And so on and so forth.

This would have gone on indefinitely had not her Ladyship finally said to the Corregidor: 'Be quiet, now! Our own affair can wait till later. The urgent thing at this moment is to restore Tio Lucas's peace of mind—not a difficult matter, in my opinion, for I see Master Juan Lopez and Tonuelo over there straining at the leash to defend Señora Frasquita.'

'I don't need men to defend me!' stoutly maintained that lady. 'I have two much more trustworthy witnesses whom nobody can say I bribed or suborned.'

'Where are they?' asked the Miller.

'Downstairs, at the main door.'

'Have them come up—with her Ladyship's permission!'

'The poor dears aren't able to come up.'

'Ah! Two women, eh? There's fine evidence for you!'

'They aren't women. They're just two little asses.'

'Worse and worse! Two lasses! Oblige me with their names!'

'One is called Pinona and the other Liviana!'

'Our two donkeys! Frasquita, are you joking with me?'

'No, I am very serious. I can prove by the testimony of these asses that I was not at the mill when you saw the Lord Corregidor there!'

'For Heaven's sake, explain!'

'Listen, Lucas, and die of shame for ever having doubted me! While you were coming back tonight from the village to our house I was on my way from our house to the village. And so we passed each other on the road! You were off the road—as a matter of fact, you had stopped to strike a light in a ploughed field!'

'That's true—I did stop! Go on!'

'Just then your ass brayed. . . .'

'It did indeed!—Oh, I feel so happy! Go on! Go on! Every word you speak gives me another year of life!'

'And that bray was answered by another animal from the road. . . .'

'Yes! Yes! Yes! God bless you! I can hear it now!'

'It was Liviana and Pinona recognising each other and saying "Hallo!" like two old cronies—while we ourselves not only didn't exchange greetings but didn't know each other from Adam!'

'Say no more! Say no more!'

'Not only did we not know each other', went on Frasquita, 'but we took fright and went scurrying off in opposite directions. . . . So you see I wasn't at the mill! If you want to know why you found my Lord Corregidor in our bed, feel those clothes on you which are still damp, and they will tell you better than any words from me. His Lordship fell into the millstream, and Weasel undressed him and put him to bed at the mill. If you want to know why I opened the door, it was because I thought it was you drowning and crying out to me. Finally, if you want to know the whole story of the appointment—however, I've nothing more to say at present. When we are on our own I'll enlighten you on this and other particulars that I must not mention to this lady's face.'

'Everything Señora Frasquita has said is Gospel truth!' Master Juan Lopez cried, eager to ingratiate himself with the Lady Mercedes, since he judged her to wear the trousers in the Corregidor's household.

'Yes, everything! Everything!' echoed Tonuelo.

'Everything—as far as you've gone!' the Corregidor assented, very relieved to find that Frasquita's explanations had not gone very deep into things.

'So then you are innocent!' cried Tio Lucas, completely convinced by the evidence. 'My Frasquita! Frasquita my beloved! Forgive me for being so unjust! Let me kiss you!'

'That's quite another kettle of fish!' his wife retorted, drawing back. 'Before there's anything of that I must hear what *you* have to say for yourself!'

Here the Lady Mercedes quietly interposed: 'I'll speak for him and for myself.'

'This is what I've been waiting for this past hour!' snorted the Corregidor, trying to draw himself up to his full height.

'But I won't utter a word', her Ladyship went on, 'till these gentlemen have changed back into their own clothes . . . and even then I'll only speak to those who deserve to hear!'

'Here! Come and change clothes', Lucas said to his Lordship, relieved now that he had not killed him, although feeling for him a really savage hatred.

'Your Lordship's jacket is strangling me. I've been most uncomfortable all the time I've had it on.'

'You don't know the way of it!' growled the Corregidor. 'For my part, I can't wait to put it on again and then have you—yes, and certain others— strung up on the gallows if my wife's defence is not to my taste!'

Her Ladyship smiled at this and gave the company a look intended to say to anyone whose fear had been renewed by the Corregidor's threat: 'Take no notice of *him*! I'll see you come to no harm.'

CHAPTER XXXIV

The Governor's Lady is Inviting Too

ONCE the Corregidor and Tio Lucas had gone from the room her Ladyship sat down on the sofa, made Señora Frasquita sit beside her, and, turning to the servants and retainers cluttering up the doorway, said with a pleasant naturalness: 'Now my friends! Tell this gracious lady all the bad things you know about me.'

The whole group moved forward as one man, and ten voices would have spoken at once, had not the nurse, as the leading spirit below-stairs, imposed silence on the others and begun herself: 'You must know, Señora Frasquita, that my Lady and I were busy tonight looking after the children, waiting for the master to come home and telling our rosaries three times over to while away the time. Weasel had told us that my Lord Corregidor had gone out after the most bloodthirsty criminals and there couldn't be any question of going to bed till we'd seen him come home safe and sound. And then we heard a noise made by somebody in the very next room— the one my lord and lady sleep in! We picked up the lamp—we were scared clean out of our wits!—and went to see who it was moving about there. And, Holy Virgin! on getting into the room we saw a man dressed

124

just like his lordship trying to hide under the bed!
But it wasn't his lordship at all—it was your husband,
Señora! At that we all came out with "Thief!
Thief!" In a twinkling the room was full of people
—and the Alguacils made a grab at the impostor
and dragged him out of his hiding-place. My Lady,
who, like all the rest of us, recognised Tio Lucas and,
seeing what clothes he was wearing, was afraid he
had made away with the rightful owner, started
weeping and wailing in a way fit to melt a stone
statue. "Throw him in the cells—the cells!" we all
kept shouting. I tell you, "thief" and "murderer"
were the kindest words Tio Lucas had thrown at
him from start to finish. So then, there he was,
looking like death, cowering against the wall with
never a word to say for himself. When he realised they
were dragging him off to the dungeon he ups and
tells us—yes, I'll tell you what he said, though I'm
sure he'd have better held his tongue. "Your Ladyship", says he, "I'm not a thief nor a murderer. The
real thief and murderer—at any rate, he has murdered my honour—(those were the words he used)—
is in my house—in bed with my wife"!'

'Poor Lucas!' sighed Señora Frasquita.

'Poor me!' murmured her Ladyship.

'That's what we all said', went on the nurse.
' "Poor Lucas—poor Ladyship—poor Lady Mercedes!" The fact is, Señora, we had a notion that my
Lord had his eye on you . . . though nobody dreamed
that you—'

'Now then, Nurse!' her Ladyship sharply inter-
vened. 'No more of that, if you please!'

'I'll go on from here', broke in one of the Alguacils, profiting by the interruption to take the centre of the stage. 'Tio Lucas—after taking us all in nicely with his suit and way of walking as he entered the building —so much so that we all took him for the real Corregidor—hadn't come with the best of intentions, and if her Ladyship hadn't still been up . . . well, you can imagine what would have happened.'

'Get along with you! Hold your tongue now!' the cook interrupted. 'You're just talking a lot of nonsense! Now, Señora Frasquita! Tio Lucas, to explain what he was doing in my mistress's room, had to own up to his real intentions. To be sure, my Lady couldn't contain herself when she heard what they were! So she gave him a good slap on the mouth and knocked the rest of his words down his throat. I too called him all the names I could lay my tongue to and would have scratched his eyes out . . . for—look you, Señora Frasquita, though he is your husband, the idea of coming here on purpose to—!'

'You're a windbag!' growled the doorkeeper, thrusting himself in front of her. 'You'd be delighted if it happened to you! Briefly, Señora, listen to me and we'll come to the facts. Her Ladyship did and said everything most dignified and proper, then afterwards, when her anger was out, she felt sorry for Tio Lucas and, coming to a full sense of the Corregidor's wickedness, she said to him at last in so many words: "Infamous as what you had in mind was, Tio Lucas, and though I can never pardon such an affront, it is necessary, nevertheless, that your wife and my husband should believe for the space of a few hours that they've been treated to a dose of their own bitter medicine, and that you, by the help of the disguise you are wearing, have given injury for injury. No better revenge can we take upon them than this little deception. We can undo it whenever it suits us." Once her Ladyship and Tio Lucas had agreed on this they rehearsed the lot of us in everything we should say and do when his Lordship returned, and certainly my stick has so taken it out of Master Sebastian Weasel's backside that it'll be a long time indeed before he forgets the eve of St Simon and St Jude!'

For some time after the doorman ended her Ladyship and Frasquita went on whispering and muttering to each other, pausing every now and again to kiss or break into merry laughter. It was a pity that their conversation could not be overheard. The reader, however, will easily imagine it for himself. Or if he cannot his good lady certainly will.

CHAPTER XXXV

Imperial Decree

Just then the Corregidor and Tio Lucas came back into the room, each now dressed in his own clothes.

'Now my turn has come!' the Corregidor announced, and, after he had thumped the ground a couple of times with his bamboo cane as though to reassure himself by the feel of it, he said to her Ladyship with amazing coolness and deliberation: 'My dear Mercedes! I am still awaiting your explanations!'

Meanwhile Frasquita had got up from her chair and given Lucas a little pinch of reconciliation. It fairly made him wince, but at the same time she gave him a fond and totally forgiving look. The Corregidor could not fail to notice this little byplay but stood, stony-faced, unable to make anything of it. Then, turning once more on his wife, with acid politeness, 'Madam', he said, 'everybody is coming to an understanding except ourselves. Take me out of my uncertainty! . . . I command you as your husband and your Corregidor!' And he gave the ground another dig with his bamboo.

'So you are leaving us?' said her Ladyship. She went up to Frasquita, completely ignoring his Lordship. 'You need have no fear that this scandalous affair will have any unpleasant consequences. Rosa! Lights for Master and Madam, who want to be going. . . . God be with you, Tio Lucas!'

'No!' croaked his Lordship, thrusting himself in the way. 'There'll be no going away for such as Tio Lucas! Tio Lucas shall stay under arrest till I know the whole truth! Ho, Alguacils! In the King's name!' Not one of his retainers, however, came at his call. They were all looking at her Ladyship.

'We shall see about that. Kindly let us pass!' she said, almost stepping over her husband and bidding adieu to the company with the greatest courtesy with head on one side and skirts picked up in the tips of her fingers, bowing gracefully in the act of performing the then modish reverence known as the 'pompa'.

'B-but I—but you—we—that couple—' the poor old man kept mumbling, plucking at his wife's dress and cutting short her courteous gesture. He might have spared himself—not a bit of notice was taken of him!

When everyone had gone and the estranged pair were left to themselves, her Ladyship at last deigned to address her husband—in the tone of a Tsarina of all the Russias blasting a fallen Minister with the order of perpetual exile in Siberia.

'Though you live to be a thousand you shall never know what took place in my bedroom this night. Had you been there yourself, as you should have been, you would not need to ask. As far as I am concerned, there is absolutely no reason—there never will be— why I should satisfy your curiosity. I despise you so much that, were you not the father of my children, I should thrust you out of this window here and now —even as I now banish you for ever from my bed. And so, sir, a long good-night to you!'

With these words, which Don Eugenio listened to wide-eyed—left alone with his wife he was no bolder than a rabbit—her Ladyship strode out into her boudoir and from her boudoir passed into her bedroom, closing the door behind her. The poor man stayed behind in the centre of the salon floor, as though rooted there, and muttered between his teeth, or rather gums—for teeth he had none: 'Gad, I didn't expect to come out of it so cheaply! Weasel shall find me a berth to lie in!'

CHAPTER XXXVI

Conclusion, Moral, and Epilogue

THE dawn chorus of birds was in full song when Tio Lucas and Señora Frasquita left the city for their mill. Both man and wife went on foot and before them ambled, ready-saddled, the two asses. 'On Sunday you must go and confess', Frasquita was saying. 'You must cleanse yourself of all the evil thoughts and wicked intents of last night.'

'You are right!' agreed the Miller. 'But you too, you must do something for me in return, and that is —give those mattresses and bedclothes away! Let's have everything new! I'm not laying myself down in the place where that poisonous beast has sweated.'

'Don't mention him, Lucas!' Frasquita broke in. 'Come, let's talk of other things. I want to ask you a second favour—'

'Do, my dear!'

'Next summer do take me away to try the waters at Solan de Cabras.'

'For what reason?'

'To find out whether we shall have children.'

'A happy thought! I'll certainly take you there, God willing!'

Here they arrived back at the mill, just as the sun,

still hidden below the horizon, was gilding the peaks of the mountains.

*   *   *

That evening, to the great surprise of man and wife, who were not expecting any more visits from people of quality after a scandal like the previous night's, there flocked to the mill a greater number of the gentry than ever. The reverend Bishop, a large number of Canons, the learned Doctor of Law, two Priors, and various other gentlemen—commanded or coaxed to come by his Reverence as soon as the affair became public knowledge—were in bodily occupation of the little vine arbour.

There was only one absentee—the Corregidor.

Once the company was fairly met, my Lord Bishop made a little speech. In spite, he said, of certain recent happenings at that house, his Canons and he would continue to come there just as before, so that neither the good Miller nor his lady nor anybody else in his audience should share the general censure —which was only deserved by the one who had profaned such a chaste and honourable marriage by his disgraceful conduct. In fatherly fashion he exhorted Señora Frasquita to be less provoking in the future, a little less—so to speak—coquettish in her speech and looks, to try to wear a little more on her arms and shoulders, and to affect a higher neckline. He recommended Tio Lucas to be a little less mercenary, to have a little more restraint and less forwardness in his dealings with his betters. In conclusion, he gave the whole company his blessing and announced that, as he was not then fasting, he would eat a bunch or two of grapes with much pleasure. The company concurred in his remarks—particularly in the last one. The vine hardly stopped quivering the whole evening. That night's entertainment cost the Miller fifty pounds of grapes, as he was never tired afterwards of telling.

* * *

For nearly three years those delightful evenings continued—until, contrary to everybody's expectation, Napoleon's armies burst into Spain, and the Peninsular War broke out. The Lord Bishop, both the Canons—the Magistral and the Penitentiary—died in the year '08, and the learned Doctor and all the other habitués at those social gatherings in the years '09, '10, and '11, from sheer inability to bear the sight of Frenchmen, Poles, and other foreign invaders smoking their pipes in the side-aisles of the churches while Mass was being said for the troops.

The Corregidor, who never again visited the mill, was deposed by a French Marshal and died in prison at the Royal Palace for being unwilling—be it said to his undying credit—to treat for a single moment with a foreign régime.

Dona Mercedes never remarried. She gave all her children an excellent education and withdrew in her old age to a convent where she ended her days in the odour of sanctity.

Weasel went over to the French.

Master Juan Lopez turned guerilla and led a band. He fell, together with his Alguacil, at the glorious battle of Baza after having personally accounted for many a Frenchman.

Finally, Tio Lucas and Señora Frasquita, though they never had children for all their trip to Solan de Cabras and their endless vows and petitions, continued to love each other as much as ever and reached a very advanced age, having witnessed the passing of the absolute monarchy in 1812 and 1820 and its reappearance in 1814 and 1823, until at length the constitutional system was well and truly established with the death of the absolute King; then they passed to a better life—it was just on the outbreak of the Seven Years' Civil War—though the beaver hats that everybody affected in those days never banished from their memories the grand old times symbolised by the Three-Cornered Hat.